WILLIAM PELFREY worked his way through Wayne State University as a law clerk and construction laborer. One month after graduation he volunteered for the draft and was sent to Vietnam. There he served as an infantryman for a year in the Central Highlands.

THE BIG V

WILLIAM PELFREY

AVON
PUBLISHERS OF BARD, CAMELOT, DISCUS AND FLARE BOOKS

AVON BOOKS
A division of
The Hearst Corporation
1790 Broadway
New York, New York 10019

Published by arrangement with Liveright
Publishing Company
Library of Congress Catalog Card Number: 83-91196
ISBN: 0-380-67074-7

First Avon Printing, January, 1984

Printed in the U. S. A.

WFH 10 9 8 7 6 5 4 3 2 1

For Jim and Bernie,
who made it back; and
Tommy and LeVon, who didn't.

CHAPTER ONE

The night we packed our duffle bags to leave Fort Polk two guys remarked that at least they were flying us over in a civilian jet, with stewardesses. I just kept packing. A civilian plane was just another form of harassment, only exceptionally cunning since most guys in the infantry really would see it as a favor. Now that the whole thing's over though, I can look back and say that if it happened again I would be pragmatic—not simply naive like most, in fact more bitter than I was, only not brooding—and be immediately thankful to fly in a civilian jet.

The head stewardess on my plane was a redhead. Everyone eyeballed her, and when she bent over to pick up a milk carton it turned out that she wore a dipping pink-flowered brassiere. When we landed she pranced, straight-backed, to the front of the plane, scraping each seat with her long fingernails. Before the lifers took command she smiled into the microphone: "Welcome to Cam Ranh Bay, gentlemen. We'll see you all in 363 days. It's been a pleasure having you aboard, and on behalf of the entire crew I hope you've had a pleasant flight."

Pleasant flight. I sat there in new jungle fatigues, trying to picture the smiling Pentagon lifer who had thought of flying us over on a civilian jet, with that farewell speech from a redhead. What a coup in the annals of harassment.

We got off the plane and stood sweltering on the concrete for half an hour before buses came. Cam Ranh Bay. No dinks lurking behind elephant grass, no steaming jungles or flaming napalm; just white concrete, a few C-130s lined at one end. The only thing even near the combat zone of television news was the heat, rippling the air in front of you. There were some rusting coils of concertina wire at the air field's edges, an un-manned bunker at each corner, but that was all, and Fort Polk, Louisiana, had had both.

When the buses did come an E-7 with spit-shined jungle boots, starched fatigues, and no CIB took charge. The officers and senior NCOs left on the first bus, and the E-7 started yelling, trying to rush us just like the first night of basic training.

Everything at Cam Ranh Bay turned out to be that way, customs check, bedding issue, police calls. I don't know why, even the lifers couldn't expect you to pay attention to that kind of harassment at this stage. I deliberately ignored a staff sergeant who called me a shit-bird and told me to pick up a piece of cellophane on police call.

The lights burned all night in the barracks, guys played radios, and a loud speaker announced mandatory formations every few hours. I lay in a top bunk all the time, cursing the whole world, just like in a movie.

We left Cam Ranh Bay the second night. At the shipping formation they sent us to a bulletin board showing the base camps of all units, below each place a list of troops going there. It was actually violent with everyone pushing to check for his name. The tension mounted as I moved from list to list. Finally, Pleiku, very last man.

I was elated. Pleiku meant the Fourth Division, the Central Highlands, and all instructors at Fort Polk had said that the Central Highlands were slackening in action. My worst fear had been of going to the infamous First Cav or 101st Airborne.

At midnight we took off for Pleiku Air Base on a C-130 with no seats. The plane made classic Hollywood grinds and squeals, water dripping from overhead pipes and steam hissing from valves on the walls. I know I wasn't the only one eyeballing the ceiling for emergency evacuation procedures, sitting there on the duffle bag.

We arrived at four in the morning. The terminal was closed, so we all lay down on the gravel yard. It was a clear night, much cooler than Cam Ranh. I was feeling easy, having averted the 101st, and went right to sleep. Just like that, in the middle of God-knew-where. I heard artillery and saw red tracers streak into a hill, but I didn't think about it. That's the way it is in the Big V. If I had pictured tracer rounds and artillery going off at Fort Polk I would have been apprehensive, but when the situation arises you don't think about it. The target must have been two clicks from us anyway.

In the morning another E-7 with starched fatigues and spit-shined jungle boots yelled us onto the bus for Camp Enari. I still saw no M-16s, no steel pots, nothing to suggest a real combat zone. Thinking of it on the bus I took heart, maybe it wouldn't be that bad. I had all along maintained hope of getting out of the infantry. At Fort Polk I had gotten a secondary classification as a French interpreter. I had a B.A. in history and a letter from a professor who had been a captain in Korea; maybe going to Pleiku was only the beginning of good luck.

With hindsight I would of course never again delude myself. Never delude yourself about anything.

CHAPTER TWO

At Camp Enari we went through a miniature jungle school for a week before final assignment to a unit—basically it amounted to intensified police calls and work details while they determined our final and specific fate. The third day we were given our assignment and the unit's armorer came to issue weapons and gas masks. Next day we zeroed-in, and the last day was a phony instructional patrol a few hundred meters outside base camp.

I was the only one to go to the First of the Twenty-second. The mail clerk picked me up in a jeep. When we reached the battalion he told me to wait outside the orderly room. I sat on my duffle bag watching the helicopters—our battalion area was right in back of the pads. Coming down they blended with the hazed mountains, beating flat and muffled beyond the blue—infantry blue—buildings.

Another clerk came out with a slate in his hand.

"Winsted?"

"Yes."

"You're goin to Echo company. Your clerk's at the snack bar, take your sixteen to the arms room and come right back. I'll take care of you."

I left the duffle bag and gas mask on the gravel and checked my rifle in with the armorer. There were plank walks connecting all the blue buildings, like the walks in Hollywood westerns. I glanced at the flag pole and its chain fence on my way back to the orderly room.

First thing you see when you enter the orderly room is the painting, "Those are *Regulars,* by God."

It was a famous painting, one of a series of five or six, honoring decorated units and hung in all Army mess halls back in the states. "Regulars." It was a battle in the War of 1812, the battalion was charging a hill in rag-tag civilian clothes, the commander thundering to a skeptic, "Those are *Regulars,* by God." The First of the Twenty-second had also been in five Indian campaigns, including the second battle at Little Bighorn, where Custer was avenged. We were also the prime strike force in suppressing Aguinaldo in the Philippines, first ashore at Utah Beach, and first to penetrate German soil in 1945.

"You a grunt?" the clerk asked, annoyed at my interruption of his *Playboy.*

"Grunt?"

He picked up the slate and leaned back in his chair.

"What's your MOS?"

"11B1L27."

"What the fuck's an L27?"

"Qualified French interpreter."

He laughed. "You're a grunt, pal."

Grunt. Smiling as he said it. He actually grunted the word.

"Hey Welch," he yelled to a buck sergeant, "got your new pack." He dropped the slate on top of *Playboy* and left.

Welch actually had a CIB, first one I had seen in Vietnam. CIB is the Combat Infantryman Badge, awarded after your first fire fight. He smiled and shook my hand before sitting down.

"Winsted?"

"Right."

"Welch. I'm your company clerk. You're eleven bravo, right?"

"11B1L27."

He moved his eyebrows but didn't ask what an L27 was.

"Right. Well, Echo company consists of four-deuce mortars and battalion recon. You know what a four-deuce is?"

"Vaguely."

"Don't worry," smiling. "Just between us I think Captain Granger's gonna put you in four-deuce. They're way below strength, and there haven't been any eleven charlies comin in."

"Four-deuce sure beats humpin the boonies," I said. I knew enough about mortars to know that a four-deuce is too heavy to carry on your back and therefore stays on secured fire bases.

"But I can't tell you for sure," glancing down at the slate. There was an index card on top with my name and serial number.

"You don't have any college, do you?"

"B.A. in history."

"You've got a degree?"

"That's right."

He shook his head and wrote on the card.

"Is that bad?"

"You know what an RTO is?"

At Fort Polk RTO and machine gunner were the two supreme dreads. The drill sergeants had emphasized that RTO takes more intelligence than any other job. RTO, radio-telephone operator.

"What's an RTO got to do with four-deuce?"

"We've got a forward observer and RTO attached to each rifle company. Captain Granger'll tell you where you're goin."

"You think he's gonna make me an RTO?"

He shook his head again and eyeballed me. "Fuck me, buddy, You're a goddamned grunt anyway. Captain Granger'll talk to you. Meantime I need your next of kin and some other happy horse shit."

Next of kin. I told him, just like in stateside sergeant-PFC relationships. But at least he wasn't as outright arrogant as the first bastard. And he did have a CIB.

"Okay, Winsted. Take your gear to one of the two in-transit barracks and grab a bunk. Then take your bag and go to CIF to get your ruck sack and shit. There's a thirteen-hundred-hour formation in front of the barracks. I'll be there and take you to the captain."

As I left I glanced at the painting again. RTO. RTO, RTO, the rhythm seathed through my brain. Fuck me.

They had told us that the three prime dink targets are platoon leaders, RTOs, and machine gunners, in that order.

I balanced the duffle bag on my shouder and kicked a rock down the bare, frontier-town plank walk.

All the mattresses in the barracks were rolled up at the heads of the bunks; the only person in the building was a buck sergeant with a transistor radio. He turned the volume down as I came in.

"New fucking cruit!"

I dropped the duffle bag at the bunk next to his.

"I guess it shows."

"Brand new jungle boots. And you wouldn't carry no goddamned duffle bag if you was goin home."

"This bunk's not taken, is it?"

"Ain't none of 'em. Everybody went forward this mornin but me." The bunks were barely a foot apart; he eyeballed me, finally extended his hand.

"Tom Kell, Bravo company."

"Henry Winsted."

"Where you from?"

"Born and raised in Kentucky."

He was a shit kicker's shit kicker—that drawn face, and brogue.

"Motherfuck!" He smiled big, showing small yellow teeth. "I'm from Harlan County."

He seemed like a nice guy, open. He even looked Kentucky; long jutting chin like my grandpaw's, sunburned face, long neck, bulging Adam's apple.

"Small world," I said and sat down on the bare wire springs. "I'm from Carter County, Olive Hill. Maybe I shouldn't claim it, we moved to Detroit. I went to college up there."

"College?"

"Drafted two fuckin weeks after I graduated."

He rolled onto his back and started playing with the springs of the bunk above him.

"Well, least you didn't go to Canada like the other characters."

I didn't see anything wrong with Kell back then; I just wasn't in the mood for talking and making buddies. RTO.

All the illusions of manipulating my way out of the infantry and having been lucky to get in the Fourth Division were rapidly fading. I told him I would see him later.

"You bet, Kentucky."

While they got my ruck sack and other gear ready in CIF they sent me to the baggage room. I left everything in storage except my pad of writing paper. I had brought several paperbacks but was too numbed to think about reading. When I returned to the baggage room to go home I gave the duffle bag to a gook KP without even opening it.

By the time I got through hassling at CIF it was time for lunch. The clerks were in a hurry to eat, shoved everything but the ruck sack into a waterproof bag and yelled me out the door.

I threw it all on the bare wire springs of my bunk. Kell was gone.

I don't remember my first meal as a Regular, just the wood-panelled walls, decorated with plaques of the patches of all combat divisions in Vietnam. The chairs had infantry-blue covers on the backs, with the battalion crest. Our crest was a shield with the sun god rising above a castle wall, symbol of the Philippine campaign; five arrows pierced through the sun god for the five Indian campaigns. They had gook KPs serving officers and senior NCOs like in a restaurant, and everybody seemed to be a permanent base camp clerk—clean starched fatigues and polished boots.

At the formation Welch pulled me out before the first sergeant arrived. He said if I stayed I'd get a work detail as soon as I finished with the captain, maybe even bunker guard that night. He escorted me through the back of the ranks and across the gravel, past the flagpole memorial with its black chain fence.

Captain Granger was sitting on Welch's desk looking at his *Playboy.*

"This is our man, sir."

"Winsted?"

"Yes, sir."

"Better get back to the formation, Welch."

"Yes, sir."

"Welcome to the First of the Twenty-second, Winsted."

CIB and airborne wings. It's funny, looking back, whenever I met somebody I would instinctively glance at the left pocket for the CIB. I still do whenever they show a soldier on the news. I guess in my belief system, or whatever, you can't call yourself a real soldier without a CIB. And you *can't*. Problem is, some guys get CIBs without ever going through any real shit.

As he put the magazine down I saw the Special Forces patch on his right shoulder. A patch on the right shoulder means you've served a combat tour with that unit. Green Beret captain on his second tour in the Nam. Fuck me, I thought.

"Come on, I'll open the Old Regulars' Inn and we'll drink while we talk."

That set me back. And he didn't look like a lifer. He wore narrow wire-framed glasses—in basic a drill sergeant had called a guy a shit-bird hippy for wearing wire-framed glasses and made him low-crawl on the asphalt yelling "Fuck the hippies! Fuck the hippies!"

I had characterized all lifers as making it their prime mission to uphold the Hollywood image of virility and superiority, but he looked natural and human—like he didn't care to hide the fact.

I guess Captain Granger almost had the US attitude—US is conscript as opposed to RA, Regular Army. He didn't give a fuck, except when he had to cover his ass, and no one with rank can survive without covering his own ass with the other lifers.

He had a sunburned face, like Kell. His nose was peeling; wavy black hair instead of the weekly crew cut, and small blue eyes. Thin mouth, straight and unemotional, but the hardness looked closer to character than to military bearing. I had never pictured myself drinking with a lifer. But he still had that Special Forces patch on his right sleeve.

The Old Regulars' Inn was a private club for the battalion. It was locked, but he had a key.

Again the painting. This one had a fancier frame. "Regulars by God." Conscripts by fuck.

It hung above the bar, I eyeballed it as the captain pulled out two glasses and put ice in them. He poured each with Jim Beam and coke.

"You've got a degree?"

"Yes, sir. History."

We sat down at the first table. "Where'd you go to school?"

"Wayne."

"In Detroit?"

"Yes, sir."

He nodded and lit a thin cigar. He offered me one but I shook my head.

"I went to Syracuse. Economics."

Fuck me, I thought. A degree and a career soldier, infantry.

"Echo company's unique from the other four rifle companies. We have four-deuce and recon, and that's it."

"Yes, sir, the clerk told me."

"Oh. Good." Clearing his throat, "You're a grunt, Winsted, but you're luckin out. I'm gonna make you a four-deuce RTO."

Just like that. "Luckin out."

He paused, blowing smoke rings, then took a drink.

"You don't know anything about adjusting indirect fire, do you?"

"No, sir."

"No sweat. You'll learn. At first all you'll do is watch your FO and get used to the radio. In three or four months you'll be an FO yourself and have your own RTO. Should also make E-5 quicker than in a rifle company."

As if E-5 stripes meant anything.

"We have an FO team attached to each company. You'll be going to Bravo."

I thought of Kell.

"Fi Bait'll be your FO. You'll get along well with him. He's got his shit together; just listen to what he tells you. He's got a degree in history, too. In fact he's a Phi Beta Kappa."

He drank again. "You'll go forward with the convoy to

LZ Clarissa tomorrow morning, catch a bird from there to Jude."

"Jude?"

"I should have covered that. Bravo company's set up on LZ Jude. The battalion's working the tri-border. Jude's on a mountain two clicks from Cambodia."

Fuck me, Cambodia.

He had been staring in his drink. The reflection streaked his wire-framed glasses as he lifted his head. "You actually picked a good time to go out. Lucky thing you didn't come in at the start of a search and destroy."

He drank and slid the emptied glass from hand to hand across the table, staring down.

"You're probably nervous now, but you'll do all right. Every college man I've ever seen over here adjusts quicker and comes through better than the others. Especially in a fire fight. I try to make it SOP for all my FO personnel to have degrees."

I said nothing. SOP is standard operating procedure. He talked just like a lifer at a briefing. Confident, precise, only deliberately avoiding looking at me, playing with the glass as he talked.

"You can have this afternoon free. Be a good idea to stay out of the battalion area; if the first sergeant sees you he'll nail you with a detail."

"Yes, sir."

He smiled. "Don't worry. Just keep a cool head. You'll find out that if you just forget all that stateside happy horse shit, just take it as it comes and be yourself, it's bearable."

"Yes, sir."

As I went down the plank walk he yelled to me, "By the way, you might talk to Welch. He used to be Fi Bait's FO."

I never talked to Welch again. That afternoon I went back to the barracks, convinced that I had gotten the royal shaft. Why *didn't* I go to motherfucking Canada? Or Sweden? Motherfucking United States. Why not some smart-ass that deserved it, why not a goddamned rich kid, or a hippy? Kiss my ass.

Kell was in the barracks.

"Henry boy!"

I rolled my eyeballs back into my skull hearing the voice, squealing, unpretentious, eastern Kentucky.

I went straight to my bunk, threw the gear on the floor, and eyeballed him.

"You say you're in Bravo company?"

"Sure am."

"I'm going to Bravo company."

"Hot *damn,*" he kicked the foot of his bunk and sat up.

"I'm gonna be the four-deuce RTO."

"Fi Bait's RTO?" His expression straightened. "Well, Fi Bait's kind of funny, but I guess he's a squared-away FO. You'll get along with him I reckon."

"Great."

"He's college, from Minnesota. Little smart-assed sometimes, but then a lot of guys are. He got a bronze star at Dak To."

"Great."

I looked at the concrete floor.

"You're lucky though. FO party don't pull bunker guard when we're on a fire base. Fuck, you don't burn shit either."

I shook my head, still looking down.

"Time'll pass quick if you don't mope about it. Keep your shit together and you'll make it all right."

Verbatim what they always said at Fort Polk—keep your shit together and you'll make it all right.

A beetle crawled over my jungle boot; I bent and flicked it onto its back.

"You goin forward tomorrow?"

"Yep. Reckon we'll go all the way to Jude together."

"What's Jude, anyway?"

"LZ on the Cambodian border. Beaucoup dinks."

You pronounce it boo-coo in the Big V. The beetle crawled below Kell's bunk; he stretched down, picked it up, and threw it across the room.

"That's a hard core bug." He yawned and kicked the foot of his bunk. "Henry, you got to go to Bangkok for R&R."

"You just come back from R&R?"

"Sort of. Captain Ferris swung a special seven-day leave for me. I got seven dinks last month."

Seven dinks.

I have never come so close to grabbing and shaking somebody out of the sheer need to grab and shake a body. Just grab him by the collar and shake him silly. What the hell was happening to me? RTO. Seven dinks in one month.

"Let's go to the snack bar. We hang around here and they're gonna put you on detail sure as shit."

You can't fight it.

We left the barracks and didn't get back until after six, ate supper at the snack bar. Kell told me that if I went back I'd have to make the six o'clock formation and they'd make me fill sandbags for an hour. When we returned, there were four sandbag-filling grunts who had arrived from the field that afternoon.

There was a movie at seven, a horror flick with the former blonde beauty out to do violence on the world for having had acid thrown in her face on her wedding night. I left after the first reel, passed the lighted Regulars' Memorial. Just like in a damned movie, the gleaming aluminum flagpole, floodlights on each corner of the black, chain fence, fence posts painted white, and a row of polished bronze plates on the front side of each, secured with brass nails. One plate per body: name, rank, date and place of death. Inside the fence, right of the flagpole, was a rusting cross made of welded steel engineer-stakes and wrapped in barbed wire, mounted in a bronzed .105 cannister. On the left, the Star of David, same rusting steel and also wreathed in barbed wire. The floodlights converged on the flagpole's white stone base. A polished bronze plate with deeply cut letters:

To our Dead Comrades,

REGULARS BY GOD,

Lord may these

brave men

Rest in Peace.

There was a breeze blowing; I glanced up and down the plates on two of the fence posts. Kontum, Dak To, Ban Me Thuot. I recognized the places from television.

CHAPTER THREE

It was still dark at the reveille formation. Beating helicopters used the strobe lights under their noses to come down behind us. The first sergeant had to raise his voice. After the formation I went to chow alone; Kell went back to the barracks to sleep.

I woke him at seven-thirty and we went to the arms room together. I drew my M-16 and three bandoliers; he had a grenade launcher and nylon vest with pockets for the rounds. He had taped his name to the fiberglass stock, "Sergeant T. E. Kell." Spelled the word *sergeant*.

I also drew two frag grenades and two yellow smoke grenades. Kell helped me strap them to the pistol belt properly so the pins couldn't get snagged on a bush and detonate—he said that had happened to a guy in Delta company last month, brought the max on his young ass. He also helped me adjust the straps of the ruck frame so it would ride as high as possible on my back. If I didn't do that, the radio would kick my ass bigger than shit. It probably would anyway, humping off Jude, but you try to make it as easy as you can. I put three magazines in each pouch on the pistol belt. I tied the other two bandoliers across my chest Pancho Villa-style. Wore the steel pot low on my skull, weighted pistol belt tight and low on my hips. Combat ready. Tiger.

I really *did* feel combat ready. Real frags, live rounds all over your body, rifle. Tiger, Airborne all the way. Fuck me. I don't know.

Kell had drawn big sergeant stripes on the camouflage

cover of his helmet, in red ink. Stock of the M-79 tucked into his armpit like a hunter with a shotgun, short barrel broken open. He grabbed his faded ruck sack and we were off. The leather fronts of his jungle boots were scuffed white. I felt embarrassed, walking behind him, new cruit written all over me.

A deuce-and-a-half was waiting beside the orderly room. C-rations and crates of red hand-flares were stacked level with the railings, just enough room between the tailgate for us to stretch out on the floor facing each other. At least I could roll over the tailgate quickly if we were hit.

Welch came out of the orderly room with the slate, to check us off.

"All set, Winsted?"

I nodded. The barrel of my rifle rested against my shoulder.

"Be more comfortable if you take that damned ruck sack off and sit on the fucker."

I looked at him.

"What's it like to be a goddamned commando, Welch?" Kell asked.

"Sucks ass, Sergeant Kell."

Sergeant Kell. Welch had E-5 stripes himself. I looked at Kell, noting that he was sitting on the ruck. But I would wait until Welch left to take mine off.

The driver came out wearing a flak jacket; another guy with a flak jacket and a sixteen got in the cab with him.

"Take it easy, sarge," Welch yelled.

There was an oriental arch over the road as you left the battalion area, "Good luck, Regulars."

The truck jerked going through the gears; I slipped the ruck off and pushed it under me without getting up. The division LRRPs—long-range recon patrol, pronounced "lerps," the elite—were strutting towards the PX in tailored camouflage fatigues and cowboy jungle hats as we rolled toward the gates. Bright infantry-blue hat bands.

The MPs were frisking the gooks, feeling their bodies just like a policeman in a movie, before letting them in. They were mostly young girls and old men, used as KPs, waitresses, and PX cashiers. All had yellow plastic-covered ID cards pinned to their shirts and blouses. They wore the wide straw hats you see in postcards and movies; I remember being struck that they really did.

A PFC MP with a slate came to our truck and glanced over the tailgate.

"No flak jackets?"

"Didn't give us any," said Kell.

"Fuck it." He checked his slate and yelled at the driver to go.

We were out of Camp Enari. Alone. Thick brush and trees on both sides of the frayed ribbon asphalt.

"I thought we were gonna convoy," I yelled to Kell.

"We're just on our way to the convoy point. Don't worry, it'll be a convoy. Probably five miles long. Nobody goes on Highway Fourteen without a convoy."

Fuck me. Highway Fourteen. I had heard of it on television and at Fort Polk.

We reached the dirt field in five minutes and stayed there for two hours before all the vehicles were assembled and the gunship escort arrived. There was a hill with an artillery battery across from the field. First time they fired I quivered. The buck sergeant laughed.

"That was eight-inch. They bring the max, shoot twenty-three miles. I think Fi Bait called in eight-inch at Dak To."

Before our truck had come to a full stop the gooks were all over us. Mostly old men and kids.

"You buy watch . . ."

"You buy girlie pictah . . ."

"Shoe shine, numah fuckin one . . ."

Pastel silk blouses on the girls, bare feet in rubber shower thongs. Giggling and nodding their heads as they spoke. Shining black hair falling down their backs.

A kid climbed the tailgate with a shoe shine box and Kell knocked him off with the barrel of his M-79.

"Hoa, numah fuckin ten!" the kid yelled. "Cheap Charlie."

He gave Kell the finger and spat in the yellow dirt. Kell pulled an HE round from his vest and threw it at him.

"Hit the road, little fucker."

It hit him on the heel, the kid screamed but looked down and quickly picked up the M-79 round. He held it up to Kell and smiled at him before putting it in the shoe shine box, then took off running and disappeared in the crowd.

"Don't let'em sell you nothing, Henry. If you do there'll be two hundred of 'em all over the truck 'fore you know it."

Another shoe shine climbed in on my side and started shining my boot.

"Me numah one shine, Joe. Numah fuckin one."

"No want shine," I said.

He kept working. A girl saw him and ran up to the tailgate. Not over twelve or thirteen years old, the black hair shimmering to her waist. "You want buy pictah, Joe?" Smiling, white teeth and soft child's voice.

She pulled an album from the top of her blouse and opened it, leaning over the tailgate for balance.

"See."

The first picture was a GI getting a blow job from a gook girl.

"No, me no want pictah."

Kell laughed.

An old man appeared on top of the C-rations with an arm of watches, another kid climbed up with a knife.

"Me no want. Me no want," I kept saying.

Kell just shook his head. "I told you."

I started screaming, "Me no want!"

But they kept hovering, the old man with a Hollywood Ho Chi Minh beard and stub black teeth. "Numah one watch, Missah Joe," smiling big and nodding his head.

Several GIs from the other trucks had gotten down and were walking around. Two stopped below us, watching the gooks. Two more kids had climbed on; the girl was flipping through her album and pointing to each picture.

"New *fuckin* cruit," one guy yelled.

He had a joint in one hand, Remington shotgun tucked into the other arm. The steel pot was tipped back on his head, peace sign and FTA on the camouflage cover.

"Twenty-three *days*, motherfucker. I got twenty-three motherfuckin days."

The other guy laughed and pulled the shotgun trying to

move him on. My gook girl kept flipping through the album. The shoe shine was doing the second boot.

"Twenty-three days and I'm home, motherfucker. How many days *you* got? How many ya say?" leaning his ear forward. "*Fuck* you."

He threw the other guy's arm off the shotgun. The gooks stopped yapping and eyeballed him.

"You dumb fucker. You *dumb* motherfucker. You got twenty-three *lifetimes.*"

He put the joint in his mouth and let it hang on the lower lip, like a movie star would a cigarette. He walked on with the shotgun over his shoulder like a stateside troop walking guard with an M-14.

Kell kicked the shoe shine in the ass and drew the M-79 back as if to hit the old man. They scrambled down, all yelling "Numah fuckin ten." The little girl with the pictures spat and gave us the finger.

"Don't pay that guy no mind. Henry. Fucker's so high he don't know where he is. Sorry fucker. Time'll pass for you. Don't worry."

I wasn't thinking about time. Gooks. Remington shotgun, joint.

"How long have you got?" I asked.

"One-two-five. Next month I'll be a motherfuckin two-digit midget."

I hadn't thought about whores being there, though at Fort Polk you heard all the stories. Convoys were where you always got it.

They had been working all along the trucks, making sure there were no MPs around before approaching anybody. They all came to me right off, instinctively knowing the cruit. Maybe he cherry boy, maybe he pay ten dollah MPC.

"Come on, we make boom boom, Joe."

Tight American-style pants instead of the loose black pajamas the others had. That's the way you can always tell a gook whore, pants or a mini-skirt. The only one worth looking at had a pair of red Bermuda shorts.

"No want," I said.

"Hey, Mile-wide, *I* boom boom."

Kell pointed to the ugliest one in the bunch. The others put their hands over their mouths, even Mile-wide raised her eyebrows and giggled. I don't know how he could have wanted her, circular face with pudgy jowls, and flopping tits. He dropped the steel pot and vest and jumped down, keeping the M-79 and one HE round.

"Won't you get the clap?"

"Who the fuck cares, Henry boy? If I get the clap I can go back to the rear for shots."

"Come on, Joe," the others kept saying. "Me numah one girl. Numah one boom boom."

Another guy came out of the woods and his girl ran laughing to join the group.

I remember being struck that they were all so simple, even innocent about the whole thing. Soft glimmering black eyes, giggling like children.

The slender one in shorts had pallid but soft cheeks. She began moving her hands around the waist and hips. Moaning and winking.

"Oh, Joe. Mee boo-coo horny. Come on Joe." Wiggling the hips as she worked the thin fingers up under the blouse, "Me numah one, Joe. Come on."

Long shining black hair. Lips parted moaning, working the hands up to the breasts, actually squeezing the right nipple under the blouse. "Boom boom, boom boom. Me love you Joe."

The others kept giggling hysterically.

"Come on, Joe. Only five dollah MPC," whole body rolling in a belly dance, "me so horny."

She finally got pissed off with my gazing and silence, dropped the blouse and frowned, stomping the ground. She spat on the tailgate and spun around, soft shining black hair swishing across her back.

"Numah fuckin ten. Cheap Charlie."

The others screamed, slapping each other's shoulders as they moved on to better prospects.

When Kell came striding back he was still buttoning his pants.

"Worth it?" I asked.

"Shit no."

Only two more old man peddlers came by before we left; I think word got around that we weren't buying. Kell cursed and drew the M-79 back like a club before they could climb the tailgate.

The helicopters streaked up from behind the artillery hill, dropped, then buzzed us, turbines grinding, streaking, diving straight in at us. Two of them, not more than twenty feet off the ground with the fierce-looking rocket pods and mini-guns poised on each side. I ducked on that first pass. Door gunners with the big sixties.

"Hogs," Kell yelled. "They ain't nothin. Wait till you see the Cobras work out. They bring the *max.*"

The MPs sent an armored vehicle ahead of each truck. APCs, tanks, and gun trucks. Each gun truck had three quad fifties—a quad fifty is four synchronized fifty-caliber machine guns working almost like a giant mini-gun—and high steel plate all around the bed. One had "Highlander Hellions" painted on the plating, another "Aces High."

The gunships kept performing as we rolled, diving, circling, roaring. Vehicles stretched fifty feet apart, a ten-minute lapse between passes.

In places the bush had been cleared a hundred meters back from the road with stumps and black skeleton trees, like a forest fire. On some low hills you could see a tank or armored personnel carrier with cyclone fence around it to detonate in-coming RPG—rocket-propelled grenades—before they could pierce the armor. We accelerated crossing a bridge. I remember fearing it meant mines or ambush—which I suppose it could have been, but if it hadn't been my first convoy I would have thought nothing of it. There were two sandbag bunkers at each end, a sixty in each bunker and the gunners flashing the peace sign as we passed. Gook kids dove into the river on both sides. They would clutch the barbed wire, lean forward, and let go squealing. At the other end a bunch of naked kids clapped and waved at us. Some held their fingers in a V, the hand sign for "Gimme cigarette, Joe."

It was over two hours to Clarissa. Landscape monotonously serene, occasional fields of elephant grass, endless horizon hills and peaks. The rolling hills reminded me of

Kentucky, I shook my head thinking about it. Of course it was actually the triple canopy—trees sometimes a hundred feet high, hiding the bamboo groves, below that thorns and vines covering ravines and swamps and streams. Sometimes after an arc light—a B-52 strike—the bamboo is twisted and tangled so thick you can't get through. It's like hacking at steel pipe and wire, and you may have to go three or four hours to get around it.

There was a Montagnard village just outside Clarissa, with straw houses on stilts. A water buffalo stood in a mud pit in front of one house. All the kids flashed the cigarette sign; the old men stood by the entrance ladders giggling and waving. We slowed going through.

I knew we must be getting there but I hadn't pictured it as right next to a village. The wire and bunker line started immediately at the end of the village, rusting concertina stacked three coils high and tangle-foot stretched over the yellow dirt behind it, then more concertina and twenty feet of open ground before the bunkers. Every third bunker was a tower made of heavy timber, like Fort Apache except for the corrugated aluminum roof and machine gun. The MPs at the gates waved us through and we turned off from the rest of the convoy to a road parallel to Highway Fourteen.

When we reached the Regulars' area—"Regulars by God" spelled out in front of the tents in infantry-blue .105 cannisters—a guy ran out of the S-1 tent and flagged us.

"Winsted and Kell?" he yelled.

We nodded. He had spit-shined boots and no shirt, suntanned.

"You're going forward right now. Charlie company's gonna CA, gotta get you out before it starts."

Each of the lined tents had a guidon-shaped sign, infantry blue with the crossed rifles and the name of the company.

CA. Combat assault. Charlie company was milling at the pad and watched us jump from the truck. My steel pot fell off, like a first-grader dropping the chalk at the blackboard. The men standing or pacing, some with thumbs tucked into the pistol belt. One machine gunner was kneeling to tie a towel around his sixty, so he could balance it on his shoulder. Just like in a damned movie.

We sat on our packs. Kell said if we waited for the CA to finish it might take all afternoon and we'd be unable to go forward today.

But that was a futile strategy. Seven birds appeared from behind the re-supply tent area. Seven. In V-formation, their muffled beating intensified to the pitched grinding and slapping. The men jerked the packs to their shoulders and stood leaning forward, steel pots low on the skulls, holding the weapons. Just like the six o'clock news. An E-7 divided them up.

The birds went higher, closed to a straight line, and then dropped, each diving across the pad area in turn, door gunners in their green helmets with plastic microphones all flashing the peace sign. Arching at the end and circling overhead. Yellow dust whipping from the rotors when they finally set down. The men blinked, tucked their heads in, and stepped back to keep balance.

We were far enough back not to get the full sting, but we still had to squint to keep dirt out of our eyes, and the beating and shrill roar vibrated in our ears. Six men got into each bird, climbing in before the skids had touched down. The door gunners on the one directly before us helped their six with the packs, then swung the machine guns out as the engine whined piercing louder, glimmer on the windshield quivering with the jerk as the skids lifted, men with legs dangling over the sides.

They circled until the Cobras came, flitting like trained mosquitoes, in a perfect ring.

The Cobras lanced in from the east. Cobra, bringer of the max. Hump behind the tinted-glass cockpit just like the hood of a real Cobra, body only thirty-six inches wide and with rocket pods poised on each side; mini-gun under the nose, 6000 rounds per minute. Forty-millimeter cannon to cover the arch after a dive.

They only buzzed the pad once, and arched up to position as flank escort. The whole procession faded toward the hazed mountains. Flitting, trained mosquitoes.

Half of Charlie company was left standing at the pad.

They stayed there with ruck sacks on until the Cobra team shrieked in again. Fifteen minutes or so, all silent, most of the men with cross-slung machine gun rounds on their chests, just like television.

The Cobras seared your eardrums, the skids came across only three feet above the ground. They spilt in opposite arches. This time they did the circling and the slicks set down immediately. Men scrambled aboard and off to the hazed mountains in less than two minutes. Leaving the silence. There is always that unreal, total silence after a bird has left, the first voice to break it always harsh and flat.

"Them Cobras bring the *max.*"

"Yeah," I said.

We walked up to the pad man, the only other body left.

"Where you guys goin?"

"Bravo," said Kell.

"You're lucky. Got a bird goin soon as the truck brings the mail down."

It was past noon, sun high, white. I was thirsty but had only empty canteens, and I didn't want to ask the pad man. He soon grabbed the handset to answer the call anyway. "This is Zulu . . . roger, have 'em standin by."

"You guys get ready. Got an empty bird takin you up there right now."

The bird beat in before I had both arms through the ruck straps.

The pad man waved it in, backwash pushing him back squinting. Kell and I were also blown off balance; I nearly went all the way over but spun around and stepped away. Kell was already in waving me on when I turned around. I forced myself forward, leaning and holding the helmet to my skull, and climbed all the way in—fuck sitting with your legs outside. The pilot looked back to see that I was aboard and we lifted off. Just like that.

The noise seems softer inside. It vibrates and hums, almost gently, instead of the crude grinding and pounding on the ground——though you still have to talk directly into someone's ear to be heard. We followed a river with large rice fields spread off each bank. Just like on the news—

white sun was reflecting on the flooded seedling paddies and making them gleam like sections of a stained glass church window, channeling mud dikes serving as the lead joints. I watched one man plow, the big round straw hat, the water buffalo straining forward, its body purple with mud, struggling like a drugged rhinoceros you see in the game conservation films. He splashed forward and the plow jerked the farmer by the arms.

The rolling hills soon became soaring peaks and straight deep ravines—no more rice paddies. The river twisted and narrowed, at points indiscernible below the triple-canopy jungle.

Kell poked me and pointed at the purple smoke as we approached LZ Jude. We flew straight in, none of the showmanship of Clarissa. The rotors whipped the purple smoke as we came down; the pad man in his phosphorescent orange jacket waved for us to jump. The bird banked straight off the slope and faded without touching ground at all.

The pad was on a finger below the bunkers. A gate and winding, concertina-lined trail led up the hill.

"Hey, Fi Bait," Kell yelled.

I looked up the trail and saw two guys coming down. Kell passed them with a comment about Bangkok, and one guy moved behind me and lifted my ruck sack. I slid my arms out without saying a word, and he carried it up the hill for me.

"What's your degree in?" the other asked.

"How'd you know I had a degree?"

"Fuck, Captain Granger made you my RTO, didn't he?"

CHAPTER FOUR

First thing we saw going up the trail was the tripod-mounted fifty caliber, sitting on a low fighting bunker. The FO table was directly above and stood out from the sleeping bunkers.

A guy yelled from an 81 gun pit, "Hey Fi Bait, what do you hear from the French bitch?"

"She wants my dick."

"Tell her no more letters unless she promises a blow job."

Without looking at him, Fi Bait yelled back, "No blow jobs."

The guy laughed. Fi Bait guided me onto the bench. I had to duck to get under the poncho roof.

"I'm Steve Pierce and this is the Anachronism."

"Henry Winsted." I looked at the second man.

"Why do they call you the Anachronism?"

"Because that's what I *am*. You think I was born to be this motherfucker's RTO?"

"You won't be much longer, motherfucker. Where you from, Henry?"

"Detroit."

"Duluth, Minnesota. Where you from, dick head?"

"Call me Ishmael, motherfucker." Anachronism. He spread his arms like a preacher as he said it.

"The Anachronism's from motherfucking Indiana. Southern Indiana."

Not another Kell, I thought. He did evidently have a degree though, with Captain Granger's philosophy. Back then I think I did see having a degree as a favorable attribute, though now if I were to meet a perfect stranger and discover he had a degree, I would despise him right off—smart-assed college bastards.

I glanced at the PRC 25—pronounced prick twenty-five. "I was born in Kentucky myself."

"Shit kicker. You don't have the brogue," said Fi Bait.

"Neither do I," said the Anachronism. "That's college. Mother-*fuck,*" pounding the table. "Does Lifer Tom know you're from Kentucky?"

"He means young buck sergeant Kell."

"Yeah, he knows it. We came out together."

"Wow man, that's a mind-fucker." Both laughed and shook their heads.

"What do you know about a prick twenty-five?" Fi Bait asked.

"Everything you learn at Fort Polk."

"Which ain't shit," said the Anachronism.

"It's more than enough. All you need to know is how to yell 'What the fuck, over?' "

I wasn't laughing. I'm sure they both understood; they became quiet. RTO.

We watched a green-eye move down to the pad. The RTO was a stocky brother, the guy in the rear had a grenade launcher, and the leader was a buck sergeant. A green eye is a three-man team that goes out one or two clicks and sets up where the lifers think the dinks will approach if they're going to hit the LZ. The men set up by a trail or stream and hide for four nights, then another team goes down to relieve them. I remember the dried muddy clothes and expressionless faces as that first green-eye filed down. Just like in the movies, grenades strapped to their pistol belts, bandoliers across the first two's chests, third with a vest of M-79 rounds and towel around his neck. It couldn't be real, yet there you *were*. Green-eye.

"Who's your favorite character in American history?" the Anachronism asked.

I eyeballed back at him, immediately feeling on the defensive, suspecting paternal sympathy and an effort to get me talking and feeling good, or something.

"Who's your favorite character in fiction?" I asked.

"Motherfucking Ishmael!" He said it with a broad grin, pounding the table.

"I like Alexander Hamilton and Teddy Roosevelt."

"Jesus Christ," said Fi Bait.

We spent that first afternoon going on from there. The Anachronism asked me what Hamilton or TR would do with the motherfucking Nam. I told them it was a bad television serial. They laughed, but the Anachronism kept pressing, and I actually got into it.

Since the FO party were attached personnel First Sergeant Ballard couldn't make us burn shit, string wire, or go on OP or LP like the grunts. All he could do for harassment was eyeball you.

In addition to the four-deuce FO and RTO, an artillery FO with the rank of second lieutenant, a recon sergeant, and another RTO were supposed to be attached to each rifle company. But the old lieutenant for Bravo had left, and the battery didn't have another one to send, so they had taken their recon sergeant and RTO away too, leaving Fi Bait in charge of all indirect fire adjustment for the company. With no lieutenant and virtual immunity from the company's lifers we got minimal hassle. When we weren't on patrol we would sit at our table, talking, reading the *Stars and Stripes*, making new delicacies from C-ration menus. Our table was made of .105 ammo boxes, engineer stakes for legs, benches on each side made the same way, and two ponchos snapped together and stretched over a high frame like a pup tent to keep sun and rain out.

Jude was 980 meters above the valley floor. You could see both Cambodia and Laos across the valley, endless rows of hazed blue peaks. It was named after the song, "Hey Jude."

It turned out that the Anachronism was staying with Fi Bait rather than going right to Alpha company just so he could accompany me on the first patrol. They all knew it would be an ass-kicker.

We left the morning of the fourth day on a five-day recon-in-force along the tri-border. The night before Fi Bait went over re-sections on the map, using the shackle code for sending grids, all of it the kind of thing that lifers would brag at mastering but that any ten-year-old kid could comprehend, even a gook kid.

It was the first platoon's mission; they had eighteen men not counting the lieutenant and us three. Technically they should have had thirty-six plus the lieutenant and platoon sergeant. Since they had no platoon sergeant, Kell was serving that function.

Lieutenant Chivington was in charge—OCS at Fort Benning; Airborne, Ranger, a B.S. in chemistry, from Florida. He had the right attitude—at least in the bush, where it counted. He didn't like humping any more than a US. But he was still an officer, still playing their game. Young buck sergeant Kell was the only guy who liked him—and even Lieutenant Chivington didn't like Kell.

First thing that morning the Anachronism drew a case of Cs for each of us. We threw the boxes away and stacked the cans in sandbags, then strapped the tied sandbags to the rucks—this was easier than having to dig through the ruck for a meal. On Fi Bait's advice I only took one bandolier of ammo. My real job would be the radio, anyway. We kept our radio on the artillery frequency; the lieutenant had his RTO, Fleming, on the battalion Command Alpha.

We could see the thick white mist in the valley as we formed by the fifty-caliber bunker. I had the radio and two batteries in addition to my food and water, bed roll, rifle, gas mask, pistol belt with two frags and two yellow smokes and first aid packet. Fi Bait had put a plastic bag from a battery case over the handset to keep it as dry as possible, emphasizing that you always carry it over your head when crossing a stream. He also opened another battery and threw it away so I could have the bag to wrap around my wallet.

We took our packs off by the fifty and waited with the others. All were quiet. Each grunt except Fleming the RTO had two hundred rounds of glistening machine gun ammo linked across his chest, like Pancho Villa. Before I was drafted the brass shells gleaming across chests had always struck me as the most impressive detail in the television news films, the most "real." They each also had two Claymores, three pounds of C-4, and two hundred rounds of M-16 ammo.

"You guys want pills, Fi Bait?" yelled the medic.

"Who needs 'em, Phil?"

"So fuck it."

"You want one, Henry?"

"What are they?"

"Malaria pills." He walked over to me, pouring one of the white pills into the lid.

"Phil Satank, Long Island."

"Henry Winsted, Detroit." I took the small pill.

"That beats Georgia."

I soon learned that nobody but two-digit midgets took malaria pills, if you get vivax malaria it's worth fifteen days in the rear. Falcifrium malaria is fatal, but so rare that the odds of dying in a fire fight were greater than catching it, so nobody but lifers and two-digit midgets ever took the pills.

When the lieutenant made his appearance he just waved, looking at his watch, and everyone jerked the packs up. The Anachronism held mine so I could get the straps on.

A tall E-4 with a handlebar moustache walked up to the point, Remington shotgun tucked into his arm and machete in the other hand. Mastion. With the click of his shotgun everyone put a magazine in and chambered around—technically you don't chamber a round until contact is made, but we always did it before moving into the bush. Fi Bait fell in behind Fleming and Phil, then me and the Anachronism, and Big Sam's machine gun. The pad man wore the bright orange jacket, flashed the peace sign as we filed by. No one spoke or returned it.

Everyone I ever knew who had been there talked about how bad the humping was, but it's abstract when someone else talks about it. Everything is. It could never be *that* bad, None of it could.

The trail down the mountain was worn wide and slick. You could hear the point man ahead chopping over-hanging vines and limbs with his machete. The pack tortured me before we had gone a hundred meters. Taking baby steps to keep balance, straps cutting into my shoulders, breathing hard. I was soon twenty feet behind Fi Bait, with the Anachronism and everyone behind him bunched up right on my ass.

The Anachronism kept whispering to keep going. My face burned; I kept looking straight down at the ground and taking forced baby steps.

The lieutenant glanced back and saw the gap between Fi Bait and me. Everyone ahead stopped, the Anachronism poked my ass with his rifle. I looked up, saw the lieutenant, and began letting myself fall forward down the slope, grabbing passing vines and branches. I tried to dig my heels in and slide to avoid somersaulting but couldn't. Occasionally I would lunge at a bamboo clump, steel pot flopping on my head.

After an hour we had made it only a third of the way down and took a break. I let myself drop. The Anachronism gave me a C-ration fudge bar.

"Ass-kicker, ain't it?"

I didn't answer, panting, chest quivering. I could feel the grunts gazing at me, but didn't care.

"Better call in a papa lima," he said. Papa lima is army for PL, present location.

I unhooked the handset and gave it to him. Fi Bait took out the map and shackle code and they sent it in.

"Don't worry, you'll make it," Fi Bait said.

"Fuck I will."

"Have some water."

They lifted me and took a canteen off my ruck, like doctors waiting on a sick child. I didn't care. I gulped the water and Fi Bait had to jerk the canteen away.

The rain hit us before we started again. I had caught my breath and my head was clear, but I shivered in the rain. Fi Bait extended his hand I pulled myself up.

"I told you it was an ass-kicker." He took the handset and told them we were moving on.

With the rain I was able to dig my heels into the mud and slide down, grabbing passing limbs to keep my balance. I was soon able to keep up with the rest and was feeling less pain on the gentler grades as we approached the base.

The trail gradually ended and we were cutting our own way. The ground became almost level, only gentle slopes. The jungle was also thinner; we could see as far as ten feet through low bushes and sapling trees. It was still triple canopy though, specks of the dull white monsoon barely visible through the tree tops. Most of the teak woods had vines wrapped around the trunks, channeling across the ground.

We stopped for lunch in a grove of younger teak woods. Fi Bait gave me his compass and map to shoot a re-section for practice. I left the pack and climbed a tree to shoot azimuths to two distinctive peaks in opposite directions. I identified them on the map and intersected the azimuths. According to my calculations we were just two hundred meters from the river. Fi Bait agreed and had me explain where I would plot defensive targets for artillery while the Anachronism called in a new papa lima.

In my three days on Jude I had sampled every C-ration meal except ham and eggs, which everyone will warn you not to try, and had come through favoring ham and lima beans and beef with spiced sauce. I was starting my ham and limas when Kell came over, walking bow-legged and strutting in camouflage fatigues—everyone else had standard OD.

"Did you guys use C-4 to cook that?" he asked the Anachronism.

"Sure."

"Well, you know you ain't supposed to. Where'd you get it?"

"You didn't give us no heat tabs," said Fi Bait.

"CP was short on 'em. Cold Cs never killed anybody."

"You won't see the first sergeant eating cold Cs."

Kell stared at him, hands on the light stripe around his hips that the pistol belt had kept dry.

"Where'd you get the fuckin C-4?" You could tell he was serious.

"I stole it from the engineers. You gonna get me court-martialed?"

"Fi Bait, you know y'ain't supposed to cook with C-4."

"Ain't supposed to, shit! This is the fucking Nam. Why don't you give up playin army games?"

"Look, God damn it." Blushing. "Don't let me catch you cooking with C-4 *again.*"

He glanced at me as he left. You couldn't tell whether the lieutenant had ordered him to hassle us or whether he had come on his own and had just decided to drop it. Fucking Kell. Kentucky.

C-4 is plastic explosive and isn't supposed to be issued to anybody except grunts and engineers; it's an automatic Article Fifteen if you're caught cooking with it. We continued to cook with it though, and Kell never hassled us about it again, though I'm sure he couldn't help hearing the roar of the flame whenever we lit it.

We stayed at the dinner site over an hour, sitting in a perimeter and talking in low tones. By the time we got ready to move I felt better. Before we crossed the river it was level ground with elephant grass, everyone went slow and I kept up.

But the new confidence dissolved as I heard the rushing current. I'd drown in a river, big as shit. I also thought of the slimy leeches.

We trailed above the bank in elephant grass for a hundred meters, Mastion's machete making the path. The crossing was at a bend—tactically the ideal spot; you reduce the odds of being seen by half since if they're at the other end of the curve they can't see you. We passed a Rocky Mountain rapids, gushing white foam and flat jutting rocks. Just ahead of it, where we crossed, the current was slower, the drizzle hitting in calm rings on the surface.

We crossed one at a time, allowing them only one target at a time—though if you got swept away you would have to fend for yourself in the water because nobody was near enough to grab you. As I lowered myself in, I saw Fi Bait go down over his chest, rifle held above his head with both hands, like in a movie. Fuck me.

Fi Bait waited on the other side and motioned me to start. It was cold, even after being in the drizzle all day, and the current pushed hard. I shuffled my way across, feeling gently around the bigger rocks, knowing that if I stepped too high I could get swept off balance—rifle and handset over my head just like in the movies, dangling radio cord floating in front of my chest, coiled like a civilian telephone receiver cord. At the center the water reached my chin and I felt the dog tag chain float out from my fatigue shirt. I breathed deeply preparing to go all the way under, but that was the deepest point and I made it across all right. At the other side Fi Bait was smiling as I came out.

That was the last smile until supper. You never stayed smiling for long, no matter what the circumstances; there was always something dreadful ahead, and if you weren't thinking of it there was either a lifer to tell you about it or you were in the predicament before you realized it.

After the river we went two hundred meters into the bush and started crossing ridge lines. Straight up and down humping, with thorns spread among the bamboo and vines so that as I grasped to pull myself up my hands became scarred and tender, though they didn't bleed long in the rain. My pack dragged me down and sapped my breath. I kept up for ten minutes or so, then the Anachronism waved for everyone to start passing, at the same time trying to goad me on. Fi Bait came back and started the pep talk.

I kept forcing myself, guys looking around as they passed. My legs ached, my arms quivered, straining to grab the next branch.

"I can't do it."

"Yes, you can."

I finally sat down in the mud. A rifleman went up and passed the word to stop.

"Come on, God damn it. Pretty soon we'll reach the november lima." November lima was night location.

"I can't make it, Fi Bait."

"Don't be a motherfuckin pussy."

Lieutenant Chivington and Phil came down.

"What's wrong?"

"It's kickin his ass, sir. He'll be all right," said Phil. He took off his pack and unzipped the medical bag.

"Better be. Can't have no cruit slowin us down or John Wayne'll be waist-deep in my shit." John Wayne was Colonel Fetterman.

The lieutenant gave the signal for a five-minute break and sat against a teak wood, with his back to us. Kell leaned his M-79 against the tree and squatted beside him like a gook, talking and laughing.

"Take it easy, Henry." Phil poured the two salt tablets into his palm. "It don't mean nothin. Don't try to kill yourself for the goddamned army."

Fi Bait pulled a canteen from my ruck. I swallowed the pink tablets and gulped. The medic grabbed the canteen away.

"Too much water and you'll cramp. Just take it easy. Fuck it. You ain't no lifer. You don't have to prove nothin."

I nodded. "Fuck this army."

"There it is."

When we started again the Anachronism offered to trade packs but I said no. I don't know why.

As soon as we started it was the same thing. I should have refused to go unless they carried me or called in a fucking medevac.

Each step accomplished the same way, mouth hanging wide open. God, what's happening to me. My mind floated back to the world. All those smart-assed bastards in school with their daddies' money, driving their hot cars and getting the girls.

My free arm reached for anything to hold me up, body dragging, feet flapping, splashing impotently in the mud, and the muddy rifle dangling by the suitcase rear-sight handle. Girls. Those bell-bottom jeans low and tight on hips. Sweat stinging my eyes in the cold drizzle. Jeans tight, swaying hips with pink blouses that ended right under the breasts. What the *fuck* is happening to me? The smiling stewardess on the plane, bending over with the dipping pick-flowered brassiere.

My chest ached, the grunts soon started passing again.

A blonde with a short skirt and dark brown nylons. But with a smart-assed college bastard with his right arm around her waist. Fuck. That gook whore at the convoy point. My God, I should have done it. I should have *done* it.

I slipped in the mud reaching for a vine and sprawled flat, rifle in the mud beside me. It felt good to lie there, letting my lungs race under the ruck.

"I can't make it," not even looking up.

"Yes you can, God damn it."

Fi Bait and the Anachronism picked me up to a sitting position. The Anachronism took the pack off and gave me his.

That gook bitch. Tight stomach, playing with her breasts and winking. I should have *done* it.

"I don't care about the goddamned pack."

"Come on, God damn it. We only got a click to go. The worst is over."

What the fuck is happening to me? Chest covered with cold gray mud. Asian mud.

I slipped into his pack and half-rolled onto my knees, digging the rifle's stock in the mud and using it as a cane to push myself up the rest of the way. I stood swaying. The radio really did make a difference. With his pack I might be okay. I moved out. The Anachronism kept whispering behind: I was doing fine, keep it up.

Again the delirium. I kept trying to remember every beautiful girl I had ever known or seen. I began constructing the Ultimate Woman. European, slender with long hair and the Hollywood thin mouth and sparkling eyes. Myself the aloof and outlandishly rich expatriate, sitting by the pool with a two-dollar cigar. But the gook whore kept interrupting. I should have *done* it.

"This is it," said Fi Bait.

I threw off the steel pot and ruck and fell on my back in the mud, drizzle stinging my face, the ecstacy of exhaustion. I lay sprawled there until my breathing slowed. When I looked up everyone had pulled their shirts off and dropped their pants, checking for leeches.

Fi Bait waddled over to me with his pants down.

"You still wear underwear?"

I looked around. I was the only guy with underwear.

"Better jettison them motherfuckers before they roll up and rot right in your asshole. Let me check your back out."

I turned around. He said I was okay and we both dressed. One of the grunts had a big shiny one on his shoulder and Kell burned it off with a cigarette.

"Take the machete from my pack and start cutting sticks for the hootch while me and the Anachronism work up delta tangoes."

The machete was strapped directly under the flap of his ruck, on top of the Cs. It was shorter than the ones everyone else used, and with no sheathe. I watched the others cutting their poles and stakes, then started hacking at a tall bamboo.

Kell immediately ran over waving his arms, whispering not to make so much noise.

"How else you supposed to cut the shit?"

He took the machete and started chopping with short angled strokes, but soon stopped, running his fingers along the blade.

"Where'd you get this machete?"

"Why?" asked Fi Bait. He walked over to us.

"It don't look like regular issue."

"It's NVA. Welch got it at Dak To."

"NVA?" He examined it carefully. "Did you fill out a tag on it?"

"You gotta be shittin me, Kell. Tag, shit!"

"This never even was turned in, was it? You know it should have been turned in for G-2."

"Fuck me, Kell. It's only a goddamned machete."

"I don't care if it's a machine gun."

I never saw another E-5 act like that in Vietnam. Staff sergeants and above, of course; they were already lifers. But any US can make E-5. To survive, a buck sergeant has to be more like the men below him than like the lifers above him. I think Kell *wanted* to be a lifer, at least then, even if he didn't know it. He was three-year RA, Airborne Infantry. I don't know, you can't figure out if he really wanted to be John Wayne or was just fucked up in the mind or what.

Fi Bait raised his voice, "Well, kiss my ass."

Lieutenant Chivington told them both to shut up. Kell gave Fi Bait the machete and went back to work on his and the lieutenant's hootch.

The Anachronism borrowed a machete from one of the grunts, he and Fi Bait finished chopping the wood while I got the three bed rolls out and unrolled the ponchos. Mine was brand new but had been cut by thorns in several places with my free-style humping, so we used it for the floor. They beat the two poles into the ground with steel pots, tied the long center pole and snapped their two ponchos together over it. The Anachronism stretched his side and pounded the stakes himself; I stretched it on Fi Bait's side as he pounded.

As soon as we had our air mattressed blown up and the packs and rifles inside we started cooking dinner. Three pierced cracker cans for stoves. Flames roared bright orange as I lit the C-4, warming my face. I'm sure Kell heard the roar, if he couldn't see the flame.

The drizzle beat on the stretched ponchos but there were no leaks, and the rhythm made it cozy. The whole thing was so Hollywoodesque, cooking C-rations with plastic explosive in the middle of a jungle, trusty rifle by your side.

When the flames died I picked up the Anachronism's beans and meatballs with my bare fingers, cursed and jerked them back. Fi Bait gave me the match book and I used it as a pot holder.

After supper we changed socks, put the wet books back on but tied them loosely. The Anachronism passed around his can of mosquito repellent. We sprayed extra thick around the ankles, neck, and wrists.

It stopped raining at six o'clock, new sun glowing autumn-like through the wet leaves and trees. Fi Bait took his rifle and C-ration paper and went out to take a shit.

When he came back I asked how far out he had gone, he told me to tell Big Sam, the brother machine gunner behind me, and I wouldn't be shot. I only went eight or ten feet beyond Sam, behind a big teak wood. His machine gun was at the head end of his hootch, facing down the hill. As I came back he asked if everything came out all right and I smiled. Big Sam.

"See any dinks?" the Anachronism asked.

The air mattress squeaked as I rolled onto my back.

"I don't worry about seein them if they don't see me."

"How ya gonna know they don't see you if you don't see them?" asked Fi Bait.

"Fuck, if I don't get shot I'm okay. Who cares if they see my ass or not."

"Fuckin cruit's got the attitude already," said Fi Bait.

"I fear not, for Thou art with me," said the Anachronism, with arms spread, staring up at the hootch's center pole.

"With thee until the end of time," I retorted.

We were still laughing when Kell brought the grunts' radio over and told us we had the first three watches.

"Sergeant Kell, are you religious?" asked Fi Bait.

"I'm a Baptist."

The Anachronism shook his head. Kell eyeballed him but left quietly.

Fi Bait signed off from our radio and took the first watch on theirs. Our radio never left the artillery frequency, so that we could get the rounds as soon as possible if hit. I was second, and the Anachronism carried the radio back to Kell and the lieutenant for their shift when we finished.

As soon as Fi Bait signed off the Anachronism rolled over and went to sleep. I wrapped up in the damp splotch green and brown poncho liner, lying awake all through Fi Bait's watch. What an ass-kick. Yet I felt good, satisfied. I ate a C-ration fudge bar during my shift and afterwards slept like a baby.

"Get *out* that goddamned sack, motherfucker."

We were still eating breakfast when young buck sergeant Kell's martial voice rang through the jungle. Just like a drill sergeant.

"Don't call me a motherfucker you fuckin lifer."

"Wow, Kell and Mastion must be workin out," said Fi Bait.

We crawled out with C-rations in hand. I was eating

sliced beef and potatoes—beef and shrapnel in the vernacular.

Mastion's red moustache was hand-curled on the ends, he was over six feet tall and Kell looked like a clown yelling and eyeballing up to him, with the jutting jaw.

"I'll call you what I want. Everybody else is already eatin."

The Anachronism poked my ribs and nodded at Lieutenant Chivington, who came running over in his bright red Miami Beach sweatshirt. Mastion saw the lieutenant coming and pushed Kell back with one hand.

"What the fuck's goin on? You guys wanna bring all the dinks in the valley down on us?"

"Sir, everybody else is eatin and this shit-bird's still racked out."

"Sir, I don't eat breakfast so I laid back down."

"You're supposed to be up, motherfucker."

"Get off my back, you goddamned lifer!"

"You guys wanna bring motherfuckin Ho Chin Minh down on our asses?" The lieutenant screamed above them, with spread arms, then rubbed his forehead and shook his head at his own noise.

"Look Mastion, from now on when everybody else gets up you get up too. Kell, you know better than to scream in the middle of the goddamned jungle."

The buck sergeant walked away sulking. Mastion began taking down his one-man hootch.

We threw our trash on the ground, Fi Bait crawled in to make a commo check on the radio and the Anachronism began unsnapping our poncho roof.

The patrol formed in a football huddle before moving out, everyone bent forward with the packs and steel pots, talking quietly. Big Sam the machine gunner asked where my radio was.

"They made me *his* motherfuckin RTO," said the Anachronism.

"So fuck it," said Phil. "Remember, it don't mean nothin, Henry."

"Fuck it," I said.

The lieutenant checked his watch and nodded at Mastion. Mastion dropped a round in his shotgun and clicked it shut, slowly, gently. He deliberately pushed past Kell and called him a motherfucking lifer under his breath.

"Move *out,* God damn it," ordered the lieutenant.

I had thought about the humping through Fi Bait's watch and determined that I would *make* it today. It would be no sweat without the radio. They had all known the radio would be too much for me the first day, that's why the Anachronism was there. No sweat today. I would show the grunts, I would build myself up from day to day and walk back up Jude standing tall, with the radio on my back.

It was a warm and sunny morning, a few swollen water drops still hanging to leaves. But the terrain was worse than yesterday. One steep hill after another, up and down. I was soon panting, just like yesterday.

I dragged my body up, clutching the bamboo and vines. One time I just hung there, body dangling back from the straining hand, head down. The Anachronism heard my forced breath and would occasionally whisper to keep pushing, I would make it.

Right from the start we made several pauses in the march and the lieutenant and Kell would move to the head of the line. Whenever they did Fi Bait would smile back at me and I would feebly raise the rifle to signal that I was driving on.

I never considered that we were pausing to check out signs of dinks. We hadn't gone a click when Mastion ran back, waving the shotgun.

"Hit the prone, hit the prone."

Fortunately we were on a ridge with high grass and thick bush. The grunts hit the prone in a tight ring around the lieutenant, Fleming and us. I casually knelt behind Fi Bait, not even trying to comprehend.

Fi Bait looked up, saw me and waved to hit the prone. I threw myself down. I could see Sam on my left, a bush on the right blocked everyone else. I took the rifle off safe and saw my dink, just like that. Stalking through the jungle, moving straight in at me.

He had gleaming machine gun rounds across his chest like our own grunts. He wore no head gear. Baggy blue shorts, skinny-legged, carried an AK-47. His body crouched, bobbing side to side searching the bush. He couldn't have been over thirty feet away. I fired one round on semiautomatic. He body jerked erect, erect, almost like a gangster blown back by a sawed-off shotgun, only screaming, hoarse, with his mouth gaping; more like an Indian, his arms flying up and dropping the rifle.

As soon as I fired and he screamed everybody opened up. They must have fired for over a minute. I looked at Sam. He was squinting, gritting his teeth, shoulder vibrating against the blazing sixty.

When the grunts stopped the AKs were still going, that sharp popcorn-popping. You could hear the bullets whiz over your head. My God.

They started screaming and yelling commands above the shooting, you could see the grass rustle and we returned a spasm of sixteen fire. Kell's HE grenades thumped in an arc almost as fast as a three-tube mortar barrage. All the sixteens were on automatic. I glanced back, and Fi Bait and the lieutenant were in the prone yelling into their handsets.

I didn't fire any at all after my dink. I don't know why I didn't fire—looking back it's humorous.

After it was over the Anachronism asked me how it felt to get a dink the second day in the bush. That was a battalion record.

Kell said, "Feels like you're nine feet tall with a hard-on, don't it Henry boy?"

I *did* feel nine feet tall with a hard-on. A showdown between him and me, and me not only winning but maybe even saving the day for everybody, the bullets whizzing over your head, your dink bobbing back and forth in the bush.

I did though try to feel at least some kind of Baptist guilt or sorrow. I tried to picture what he must have looked like. by the way he was knocked back it must have really brought the max. At Fort Polk they had had a demonstration to show the tumbling effect of the M-16 round. The entrance hole is smaller than a dime, but as soon as it penetrates it spirals and expands. One dead dink I later saw had had the bullet enter the back of his right shoulder and somehow come out in a three-inch diameter hole in the left side of his skull. I doubt if my dink was that gory—I never saw him again; when we returned to the scene, his body had been dragged away.

That night I actually lost sleep and asked myself if I had become an inhuman animal. That dink was a human, and I wasn't even touched. His mouth gaping and vibrating with the scream as he fell back.

Human shit. If you shoot a dink. you shoot a dink. If you're dead you're dead. If someone were to dare ask me how it felt to be a killer I like to think that I would hit him in the mouth. "How do I feel?" I would *love* to hit him in the mouth.

After our second volley stopped, there was silence, and the most desperate fear I had ever felt. I remember Sam's face as three grunts threw him their sixty rounds, purple lips pressed tight together and drops of sweat suspended on his face. Total silence, all eyes fixed on the bush. Just lying there, waiting. Like in a goddamned movie.

Finally the hollow rushing, mortar rounds hitting two hundred meters in front of Sam and me—hollow, intensifying rumbling before they hit, a split-second suction before the first echoing explosion, then the steady cycle of bursts.

As soon as the first round blew, the lieutenant yelled for everybody to get up. He stood with Phil and counted as we filed passed him.

"No KIAs or WIAs, let's move out."

We took off running. I remember Fi Bait looking back over his shoulder, with the handset in his hand to give the mortars adjustments, cord stretched taut in front of the panting Anachronism.

We stopped about two hundred meters back and formed another perimeter. This time I lay inside the ring, beside the Anachronism.

Fi Bait smiled, "What did you think?"

"I got a dink."

"No shit?"

"Gunships five minutes out," the lieutenant said, loud enough for all to hear.

"Here comes phase two of the ritual," said Fi Bait. "By the time they get here there won't be a fucking dink within two clicks."

"Think it'll go to phase three?" asked the Anachronism. Phase three would be an air strike. Two or three Phantoms with napalm cannisters and two-hundred-fifty-pound HE bombs.

"I doubt it," Fi Bait said.

Kell cut a tall bamboo pole and tied a smoke grenade to one end. He climbed a tree, and when the Cobra team beat in the lieutenant pulled the pin and handed him the pole. Yellow smoke gushed above the canopy. The lieutenant relayed the position of the dinks through our TOC—tactical operations command—and the Cobras beat in lower. I looked up but couldn't see anything through the canopy.

I jumped when they started working out. The mini-guns rip and cut through the rotors' beating like amplified microphones gone haywire, a long deafening brrrt. Twelve-thousand rounds per minute, none of them distinguishable.

On the second pass they dove with rockets. The rockets scream from their pods, above the mini-guns, and slam into the terrain like artillery rounds. Pods extended and poised on each side of the narrow fuselage. The rockets leave twin brown smoke streamers behind. After the pass the forty-millimeter cannon covers the retreat, a soft patting sound as it fires, the rounds exploding in line before the patting cycle has ended.

We waited for them to expend and then formed another huddle to move back in. If the Cobras had received return fire or seen any dinks, they would have called for an artillery barrage and perhaps an air strike, but this time they saw no need to.

Sam told the lieutenant I had fired the first shot and gotten a dink.

Nine feet tall with a hard-on. I was scared, but not as scared as right after the shooting. Besides, no one really thought the dinks would still be there. Dinks know what phases two and three are.

CHAPTER FIVE

Mastion had come upon a bunker complex, bunkers dug deep and camouflaged. You would have missed them except for the gun ports. There were also one-man spider-hole fighting positions. Mastion had nearly walked into one without realizing it. After the sleek Cobras finished working out, we moved back in and found several blood trails, but no dead dinks.

Lieutenant Chivington, Kell, and Fleming the RTO called everything in to higher while we sat in a perimeter. The dinks had evidently hightailed in panic. One bunker had thirty mortar rounds with Chinese markings, another a can of Budweiser beer that Kell said was still half-full. I don't know if he drank the rest or not.

Higher said they wanted the bunkers and mortar rounds blown, but we didn't have enough C-4 and detonating cord, so they told us to go back to last night's november lima and cut a drop zone; in the morning they would send a bird with a case of C-4 and a spool of det cord.

We were elated to hear this. It was not yet noon, we could have hootches set up by two o'clock and relax all afternoon. Fi Bait pointed to the brown stained leaves of one blood trail as we reformed; I wouldn't have known it was blood if he hadn't pointed.

I felt good and grinned as we walked back. Feeling no pain, actually enjoying the feel of the ruck on my back and trusty rifle in my hands. Grenades low at my waist.

When we arrived the low skeleton frame and stakes of our hootch were still intact. The Anachronism and I unrolled the ponchos while Fi Bait called artillery liaison and told them that we would be in last night's november lima and would like the same defensive targets on call. After blowing up the air mattresses we crawled in and cleaned our rifles.

When we started to open the Cs Sam came over and asked for some C-4. Fi Bait gave him half a stick.

"Thanks, Fi Bait. Say, that's a real hard core RTO you got there," smiling at me.

"He's a lifer. From motherfucking Kentucky like Kell. Says he's gonna get sixteen dinks next month."

"Airborne all the way. At least you ain't RA, are you?"

"Conscript by God."

"All *right.*" He smiled big with even white teeth and held his hand for me to slap. His nose was pressed flat with the big nostrils, that thin coat of skin grease reflecting. "Say, I don't even know your name. I'm Sam Silton."

"Henry Winsted."

"Say Fi Bait, I'll come over and shoot the shit after while."

"Why not? We'll give you a motherfucking history lesson."

Sam was from Cleveland, twenty years old, five months left to go and intending to start college on the GI Bill when he got back. Best machine gunner in the battalion.

"Right."

After the meal we pulled our boots and socks off and lay back on the air mattresses. It felt good to wiggle the toes and hear the bones crack.

"What's the French bitch doin now, Fi Bait?"

"She's fuckin."

"You used to go with a French babe?" I asked.

"Fuck no," said the Anachronism. "He couldn't get no French broad. He couldn't get nothin."

"It's a pen pal," Fi Bait said. "I got her name from Chris Noel on the radio."

"What a *fuck.* You should see the picture she sent him. In a goddamned bikini."

"She wants my dick, I keep tellin ya."

"You got to rap about eatin her out if you really want to turn her on, Fi Bait."

"Fucking animal."

"Ain't that right, Henry? You gotta eat 'em out."

"Fi Bait don't even believe in blow jobs. Blow jobs are heaven, Fi Bait."

"Pervert."

"If you don't promise her you'll eat her out, she'll stop writin. If you rap about six-niner she'll send a motherfucking nude picture. With her legs spread on a bed and those goddamned tits cupped in her hands."

"Degrade a magnificent young woman like that. Of finest French stock."

"Magnificent young *tits.* Finest French *cunt.*"

"That's just it! Why degrade the fucking cunt? Eat her out. Blow job. You goddamned pervert."

Sam's entrance interrupted the debate. Fi Bait pulled his legs up as Sam squeezed in.

"What is this, the barefoot menagerie?" He sat on the foot of Fi Bait's air mattress, his knees propped up.

"Fi Bait still don't want a blow job, Big Sam."

"Blow job numah ten. Make baby-san only way make love."

"There it is," said Fi Bait.

"Fuck me. Tell 'em, Henry."

I shrugged. "Blow jobs are divine." Back in the world I would have blushed.

"There's my man," said the Anachronism. "You heard him, Sam."

"Fucking animals," said Fi Bait. "Maybe Alpha company'll be all perverts and he'll be at home."

"Hey, that's right," said Sam. "Pretty soon no more Anachronism."

"What do you know about Alpha, Sam?"

"Not much. CO's supposed to be gung ho."

"Fuck me."

Fi Bait laughed. "Maybe they'll square your attitude away."

"They *might,* but I fucking doubt it."

"Give me a motherfucking cigar, Fi Bait."

"Ain't got none, Sam. I should have a care package waiting when we get back, though."

"What a bummer."

"Hey, Henry here's a history man."

"He is? You been rapping with the great Phi Beta Kappa?"

"Ain't stopped since I got here," I said.

"You ain't another Anachronism, are you?"

"I'm a US."

"There it is." He extended the palm of his hand, I slapped it.

"All *right,"* he said.

"Fuck this army," said the Anachronism.

"Fuck this army," said Sam.

"Proud to serve," said Fi Bait.

"Regulars by God," I said.

"Motherfuck," said the Anachronism. "I'll go to fucking Alpha company and call willy peter in on seventeen dinks and get a direct commission. Then I'll come back here and lock Kell's heels." Willy peter is slang for white phosphorous.

"Drive on, candidate," said Fi Bait.

"Well, if you ain't got no cigars, Fi Bait, they ain't no point in me hangin around with this lifer. Where's the French bitch?"

"Left her in the bunker on Jude."

"Wow man, I'd carry that pussy with me all the time. Wrap it up in plastic, and when you start feelin sorry for yourself, like the Anachronism, just pull her out and let your dick get hard. Forget all your misery."

"Just be sure to do it in your hootch," said Fi Bait.

"There it is."

"Blow job," said the Anachronism.

"Fucking pervert."

Sam slapped Fi Bait's leg and left.

"Maintain your cool, Big Sam."

"You too, Phi Beta Kappa."

"Well, I might as well shit," I said. I put my boots on without the socks, opened the C-ration envelope for the shit paper. I also took my rifle and a magazine. When I came back the Anachronism was gone.

"Where'd he go?"

"He went over to rap with Mastion and the heads."

"Heads?"

"Heads."

I understood, but I hadn't pictured the Anachronism as that type. Heads. He didn't come back until after supper.

"How does it feel to be a combat vet?" Fi Bait asked.

"I don't know. It blows my mind."

"I know. It ain't like the movies, is it?"

"I don't know. It's weird."

"Say, you didn't see Welch when you were in base camp, did you?"

"Yeah."

"He was my FO. He freaked out at Kontum and got the clerk's job."

"Freaked out?"

"I don't mean drugs. We were goin up a hill and a B-40 hit the lieutenant in front of him. Blew the lieutenant's shit away and Welch just freaked out."

I didn't say anything.

"Just between us I think the Anachronism would freak out if he ever got in really bad shit like that."

"Where'd he get the name Anachronism?"

"I gave it to him," he said, yawning.

For supper we both had beans and meat balls and Fi Bait made a double batch of C-ration cocoa in my canteen cup, using both our cocoas and creams to make it taste closer to real cocoa. We were taking turns drinking when Kell came over.

"You guys got from one to six. Last man wakes up the lieutenant and me."

"Right," said Fi Bait. "Say, you want some cocoa? It's a double batch."

"Hell *yes,* if it's a double batch." He sat down on the Anachronism's mattress and passed the cup to me after one gulp.

"How you doin, cruit?"

I couldn't help but smile at him—the long jutting jaw, Kentucky Adam's apple, innocent brogue, and grin.

"I think I'll survive."

"That's the spirit. Kicks everybody's ass the first time. Not many guys get a dink their first patrol though. That's really somethin to be proud of."

"Ready to go back to Bangkok, sarge?" asked Fi Bait, before I could respond.

"Better believe it, boy," slapping Fi Bait's leg.

"Got any pictures?"

"Naw, ain't got no camera. I had four different gals."

"Four! Why didn't you just take six, a different one every night?"

"Fourth one I got was an angel, Fi Bait. I just couldn't leave her."

They both laughed. Kell slapped my leg. "You gotta go to Bangkok, Henry boy."

"I'll go there and get me a blow job."

Kell laughed louder. "How you gonna act, Fi Bait?"

"Not like you animals."

"Fi Bait, let me tell you, they won't *blow* you in Bangkok. And they won't let you eat 'em out either."

"Well, I'm glad someplace is still free of perversion."

"Where do you go to sixty-nine?" I asked.

"Australia," said Kell.

He looked at his watch. "I gotta go check the perimeter guard, Fi Bait. Thanks for the hot chocolate."

"No sweat, Sarge."

I could only see his legs through the open end of the hootch, strutting bowlegged in the tight camouflage fatigues.

"There goes one poor bastard."

"Why?"

"Why? He's a fuckin kid. He don't even know himself why he acts like a lifer. Fucked up in the mind."

"He's a three-year RA," I said.

"But he's a goddamned kid. He's fucking nineteen years old. Nineteen. He probably saw himself like Audie Murphy or something. He ain't the brightest guy around. Now that it ain't like the movies, it's blowin his mind."

"I met him in base camp, and before I saw him in the boonies I thought he was okay."

"He knows the fuckin bush, though."

"He told me about the seven dinks."

"That's right, seven fuckin dinks. But it's really sad. Look at all the poor bastards like him that end up lifers."

"I don't know. They can still get out."

"Where they gonna go? Where would Kell fit in the world? A janitor?"

"I guess you're right. Fucked up army."

I could see where Fi Bait may have been right. The only NCO lifers you saw were black, hillbilly, or Puerto Rican. Maybe they really took pride in their profession, Defenders of Democracy, the nation's finest; not lifers. It's really sad. Some were human, you could almost sense that they actually liked the men but couldn't show it. I bet old Sergeant Skinner was that way. And Kell.

I'm sure now that Kell had wanted to be liked all along but knew that everyone was against him because of his attitude. But if he knew everyone despised the role he played, why did he play it? Maybe that's the lifer's dilemma. Maybe they all know that everybody hates them for the role they play, not really as people; and at the same time, for some reason, they can't drop the role. Maybe even they don't know why they can't drop it. I don't know.

It was almost dark when the Anachronism returned.

"Hello, Henry my friend."

He let himself fall on the air mattress.

"Hey, Mr. Phi Beta Kappa, tell me what's gonna happen." He talked like a drunk, but with a clear and sharp voice, in a soft tone. "What the fuck's gonna become of your fucking Anachronism?"

"Go to sleep, John."

The Anachronism's real name was John Shoates. He rolled onto his back and inhaled the joint.

"Why such a fucked up world? Wow. Why, Henry?" He put his hand on my shoulder.

"Henry, what the fuck are we doin here? I mean—you're too goddamned cynical to talk about it. Motherfucking cynics. But you never wanted to kill no dink did you, Henry?"

"Keep it down, John. You don't want Kell comin over here."

"Henry, what's gonna happen when we go back to the world? How am I supposed to act? Go home and everybody'll expect you to smile. 'Our boys.' Proud to Serve."

"Go to sleep."

"What the *fuck* Fi Bait? Henry, lemme tell ya. I had an uncle in the Alamo Scouts in World War II. Fuckin Uncle Malcolm. Fucker went to Fort Polk, and he became a Baptist preacher after the war. He *cried* when I left, Henry." Inhaling, shaking his head. "Like I been tellin fuckin Mastion. I ask fucking Mastion, am I gonna grow long hair like a goddamned hippy, and stay stoned? Am I gonna become a responsible citizen of Indiana? Am I gonna join the goddamned VFW? Mother*fuck!*"

"Look John, you better get rid of the joint and go to sleep."

"Fuck you, Phi Beta Kappa. I don't give a fuck. Fuck 'em. Fuck the whole goddamned world."

Another drag on the joint. "Wow Henry. Wow. Uncle Malcolm. Hey, look at my lighter. Sam bought it for me in Pleiku. This is it."

He pulled it out of his pocket and dropped it. I rolled over and struck a match to read the inscription, cupping the flame:

WHEN I DIE BURY ME FACE DOWN, SO THE WHOLE WORLD CAN KISS MY ASS.

I picked it up and gave it back.

"There it is, Henry. There it fuckin *is.*"

"You better get some sleep. You'll need the strength for Alpha company."

"Alpha company." Shaking his head. "Alpha company can kiss my ass. Henry, you were a motherfucking Baptist. You know I believed that shit. You know what I mean? I *believed* it. My fucking father's a goddamned elder."

"I used to teach Sunday school." I don't know why I said it. I lay on my back staring at the poncho roof, regretting it.

"You did? Wow man, what a trip. Wow. You know what I mean then. I *believed* it. I'm so goddamned fucked up, Henry. I want to cry. Uncle Malcolm. Henry, you know most guys don't take it like me. Goddamned world. I'm gonna be a one-man lost generation when I get back."

"You'll go back to grad school and use that same self-pity line and get a different fuck every night," said Fi Bait. "Fucking blow jobs, too."

"Wow man." The Anachronism laughed. "Fucking blow jobs." Shaking his head.

"But it won't *mean* nothin. Look at me. Smokin goddamned marijuana. Henry, you know before I come to the Big V I never smoked marijuana. I never said the word *fuck* till the goddamned army."

I lay there, occasionally glancing at him. I thought of that grunt with the joint and shotgun back at the convoy point.

"Come on, John. I mean it. You'd better get rid of the joint and go to sleep."

"Wow. Yes, drill sergeant. A Phi Beta Kappa drill sergeant. How's that grab ya, Henry? Right by the balls? Please don't make me low-crawl, drill sergeant."

He slid forward on the mattress and flipped the joint out of the hootch.

"Mission accomplished, drill sergeant."

He shook his head and moaned. "Fucked up world," putting his hand on my shoulder, "Henry, don't look down at me. I was a motherfucking Baptist. From motherfucking Indiana. Oh God, I can't take it."

I turned away and tucked the top of the poncho liner around my neck. I was supposed to wake him for radio watch but took his shift myself. I was afraid it would be a hassle to wake him up.

We lay in the hootches until nine o'clock in the morning, birds don't start working until then. After we tore down the hootches Kell and four grunts cut a drop zone.

"Wow, was I fucked up last night."

"Do you remember what you said?"

"I do, word for word. Even Uncle Malcolm. Let me tell you, Henry, it gets to you. I'm not ashamed to admit it. Wait till time starts draggin. You're in the motherfuckin land of the *Nam.*"

"Pop yellow smoke," the lieutenant yelled.

"Smoke popped yellow," Kell yelled back.

The bird immediately beat in. It hovered above the drop zone, slapping and quivering, helmeted door gunners with their plastic microphones and nylon flight jackets, American flag on the shoulder. They kicked the C-4 and det cord and leaned out flashing the peace sign as the bird streaked off, like a race car from a dead start at the line.

One end of the C-4 crate had broken open in the fall. The lieutenant ripped it the rest of the way and distributed the sticks equally to the grunts. Kell took the spool of white det cord, the lieutenant motioned with his arms and we jerked the packs on. This time I had the radio, but like yesterday morning I resolved not to let it kick my ass. It didn't, for the short time I carried it.

When we reached the ravine Kell and Mastion collected the C-4. They walked down and put it in each bunker, Kell wrapping det cord around each packet. When they came up he motioned everybody to move out, we headed back toward the november lima and he let the det cord trail out behind him.

The lieutenant motioned for us to form a perimeter. Kell connected the blasting cap and fuse, and came skipping back through the bush like John Wayne.

The explosion blew flat and hollow, no echo or solid vibration like in the movies, all at once, dirt clods thudding around us, thick gray smoke above the ravine.

The lieutenant unhooked the handset from Fleming's shoulder strap.

"Mauler four-seven, this is Mauler five-six, over."

"Send traffic, five-six."

"Roger, bunkers blown, preparing to move on to next charlie papa, over."

I couldn't hear higher's answer but the lieutenant acknowledged, "Roger, understand. Change of mission. Will sierra-papa to your location at this time, out."

"Okay, we're goin back to Jude," he said. "I don't know what the fuck's up. Mastion, take the point. Let's make it back in time for hot chow."

It turned out that we were called back so they could put four air strikes in the terrain around the ravine next morning. When the Phantoms came you could see the show from Jude. Everyone stood on the bunkers to watch—shrieking and screaming, faint whoosh and cloud as the napalm canisters hit and spread. After they finished all eight planes buzzed Jude, diving and flitting their wings over us, firing the orange after-burners and barrel-rolling like Steve Canyon.

We took a different route back, skirting the ravines and ridges that had kicked my ass the first day. The river was a clear shallow stream where we crossed, water barely over your ankles and splashing around the boots. I breathed hard and sweated, but I didn't groan. Maybe it was the easier route.

We took a break for lunch at the base of Jude, before the slope started.

Sam smiled at me, "Ready to get your ass kicked, Kentucky?"

"You got a lifer there, Fi Bait?" asked Lieutenant Chivington.

"How'd you guess, sir?"

"Sergeant Kell wants to get rid of him, afraid of a threat to his dink record."

It felt good to have the lieutenant joke about you, like when you're a little boy and your father is talking to the gas station mechanic and refers to you.

The Anachronism took my pack as we started up.

It wasn't bad until we hit the trail. Up to that point we had moved on an angle with the slope, the full pressure of the grade deflected. But the trail was steep, twisting only when trees made it necessary. I was soon panting like the first day—self-pity, then delirium, the whole bit. The grade was so steep I almost lay prone reaching up for a lever, reaching and straining to pull the bamboo. I was soon crawling, and the Anachronism began waving people around.

Both Fi Bait and Kell came down and told me to stop and rest. Take my time going up, we had all day. The whole patrol passed and the four of us were alone in a huddle. This time I didn't even feel guilty.

"Have some water."

Kell handed me his canteen, I gulped.

"Thanks." They were all quiet as I panted.

"Ready to push on again?" Fi Bait asked after five minutes. I nodded, breathing calm by then.

"Just take your time," said Kell.

But I dropped to my knees again, crawling on all fours, the rifle slapping the ground. We had to stop two more times. The second time was at a ridge and I looked out at the valley. All the fresh green, the hazed blue mountains beyond, like a post card.

We reached Jude at least an hour behind the others. Fi Bait switched the radio to the grunt frequency and told them we were coming in so they wouldn't shoot us.

The pad man stopped us at the wire. I stood panting and bobbing, trying desperately to look dignified.

"One of you guys roster number forty-two from Echo company?"

"Me," said the Anachronism.

"You're supposed to go to Alpha company with the last bird out today."

"Mother-*fuck*. Will I still get hot chow?"

"Yeah. You'll go on the bird takin the mermites back."

"What about a radio?"

"I don't know nothin about no radio."

"Probably be waiting for you," said Fi Bait.

"Motherfuck," said the Anachronism. "Alpha company."

"Ready for the last leg, Henry?"

I nodded and made it up the concertina-lined path.

We threw the rucks on top of our sleeping bunker, Fi Bait went to the CP for mail, and the Anachronism and I sat at the table.

"Motherfuck," he said, coming back. "No care package."

"What'd I get?"

Fi Bait gave him two letters.

"Both from my mother. What a bummer."

He gave me the three copies of *Stars and Stripes.* "Sorry, Henry."

"They haven't had my address long enough for me to get mail."

"Hey Fi Bait, I'm gonna get a water can from the CP and clean up before I go."

"Okay. Take a full one, and if they hassle you, tell 'em I'll fill it from the trailer."

"When do you get clean clothes?" I asked.

"Who knows. I guess it's about every ten days."

The chow bird came in half an hour after our return. Fi Bait stayed at the table with the radio. It's SOP that when hot food comes in you carry a weapon, wear a steel pot, and stand five meters behind the next guy. If you don't, "one round'll get you all."

The line had already circled the perimeter and begun twisting around sleeping bunkers by the time they started serving. Swiss steak, mashed potatoes and gravy, and green beans, in paper plates, a quart of milk for every other man. Fi Bait met us in front of the table and took my steel pot and rifle.

"Not bad chow," I said.

"Probably won't be no seconds," said the Anachronism.

Fi Bait was one of the last in line and got half as much meat as we did—but also a full quart of milk. We stuffed the garbage into a sand bag, and I took it to the sump, which was a crater outside the wire at the south end of the perimeter.

The Anachronism was giving Fi Bait the Cs he had left over from the patrol as I came back.

"Gimme a call when you get there," Fi Bait said. "Be sure to tell 'em right away you ain't gonna burn shit or pull bunker guard. If you don't they'll treat you like a grunt."

"Right. Can't be usin that hassle."

"They got a red leg FO but I don't know what he's like. Look John, I don't want to hassle, but you better not blow any joints over there."

"Shit. What are they gonna do, send me to Vietnam?"

An RTO stuck his head out of the CP. "Hey Fi Bait, get your man ready. Bird three minutes out."

The phosphorescent pad man popped yellow smoke and stood behind it with arms raised like a football referee. The bird slapped in from the east.

"There it is," said Fi Bait. The Anachronism put his steel pot on, slung the pack on one shoulder, and carried the pistol belt and rifle in the same hand.

"Redirect my mail, Fi Bait. Tell Doc Satank I said take it easy and New York sucks ass."

"You bet."

"Good luck, Henry. Don't let it kick your ass."

"No sweat."

"If you go on R&R before I see you again, get a blow job." He tapped Fi Bait's shoulder with the rifle, grinning big.

"Move out, you fucking pervert."

The Anachronism trotted down the path with the ruck flapping against his back. Two grunts were already throwing the empty mermites onto the bird when he reached the pad. He slid in, dropped the pack behind him, and sat with his legs over the side. The helicopter banked down to the valley and dove to the floor like a gunship going in for a strike, cutting in a steep arch, fading.

CHAPTER SIX

We stayed on Jude for three more months, running recon patrols in the tri-border. Beaucoup dinks.

LZ Jude. We would sit at our poncho-roofed table all day, exempt from burning shit and pulling bunker guard. In the early evenings when it wasn't raining the brothers would gather at one of the 81 gun pits and form a singing group. They would always draw a crowd and end up doing requests. "Cloud Nine" was most popular, but they never finished without "Hey Jude," with the sun setting behind blue Cambodian peaks.

Fi Bait had a transistor radio, and we would listen to the oldies but goodies and talk of how we would act when we returned to the world. What kind of woman we would take the first night, redhead or blonde. We both agreed on slenderness but substantial tits, long legs, and a mini-skirt. Running points of debate were the proper way to curve your fingers around the cigar at the airport bar and how best to act the hardened and alienated Hollywood combat veteran, how to casually flash the gleaming CIB and crossed rifles.

I guess we knew how childish we had become, but what the fuck. I wish I could be that way again, sitting at our table, just talking, dreaming of the Life, the brothers singing at night, smoking A & C Grenadiers and discussing Fi Bait's French bitch and blow jobs. "Hey Jude."

Everything faded and blurred, the mind becoming dull, sleeping on the ground, carrying a rifle and radio through the goddamned jungle, having killed a dink. I don't know.

Cam Ranh, the plane, and redhead stewardess; Captain Granger and the Old Regulars' Inn; that first journey forward, the gook whore with her hands under the blouse; the first patrol, humping the boondocks, eating, sleeping, talking, and laughing with Fi Bait and Sam and Phil, counting the days. That was it, except for the fire fights, and you forgot one as soon as it was over; *made* yourself forget.

No Hollywood disbelief, no serious polemics except during stand down, when I was drunk anyway. Everyone had moments of brooding, especially after a KIA, but even then, it was in the context of our "environment." If you ever thought about ghastliness or misery or the horrors of war, it was with cynicism. Horrors of war, shit.

You were comfortable with your brothers-in-arms. Everyone was a buddy, we could lift each other's spirits through telepathy. Regulars by God. No one else could know what we felt. Only we knew each other's problems, *had* each other's problems.

Mail came to dominate my private existence, just like in the USO commercials. It was the one thing within immediate reach that you could look forward to, the one plausible short-range goal, the one contact with the world. I wrote to professors and people I would never have thought about as a civilian, even our preacher. A letter from the world was an occasion, no matter who it was from. I once got seven letters in one day and made a pagan ritual of opening them.

On Fi Bait's advice I asked my parents to send bouillon and dehydrated soup, also pork and beans, chile, and presweetened koolaid. My father would always throw in a can of cashew nuts, a can of chocolate pudding, and six Milky Ways with each package. That night we would have a party, like a kid's birthday. Fi Bait always got A & C cigars, and we would sit by the candle light in our sleeping bunker, like movie stars.

Technically there should be an FO on a fire base or LZ twenty-four hours a day, but on the other hand there is supposed to be one with every element in the bush. To solve the dilemma Bravo company's commanding officer, Captain Ferris, cut all patrols to three nights and four days and only sent Fi Bait and me out with every other mission.

Captain Ferris also had a partiality for the first platoon. "Best I ever saw when it comes to the bush." So he sent the first platoon on patrol more often than the second and third, just about twice as often, I guess I almost saw Lieutenant Chivington as "my" lieutenant and Kell as "'my" NCO.

I had been in-country two months and on a total of four patrols when they sent us through Plei Jan, a small Montagnard village a click from the border. The colonel, old John Wayne, said he wanted it spot-checked to see that everything was pacific and normal. Naturally, Captain Ferris decided to send the first platoon. We were supposed to stay out three nights and four days. On most patrols they give you a route of march and list of check points you're supposed to cover, but this wasn't a normal recon. Move into the village at dawn the third day, stay till noon pacifying the Montagnards with C-ration candy and medical care and then move back for Jude.

By that time the monsoon was intensifying. Every afternoon it would rain, each day a little harder and a little longer. Some days it would rain twice or drizzle all day, the valley covered with the soft white fog. It was like that the morning we moved out for Plei Jan, mist drizzle so thin you couldn't see it, couldn't distinguish the droplets striking a puddle. The whole sky was soft cotton mist. Stooped men with their steel pots and rifles silhouetted against it in classic Hollywood style as we assembled at the pad.

Mastion walked the point as usual, and Phil walked between Fleming and Fi Bait. Phil, Fi Bait, and I would exchange jokes whenever we took a break.

No matter what you said to Phil he would come back with "So fuck it," and the way he said it, the serious tone and the harsh New York voice, made you snicker every time.

Everything went all right until we reached the village, no foot trails or booby traps discovered, no contact. The second night we stopped and set up our november lima in a bamboo grove five hundred meters outside the village. It rained all day and all that night. For supper Fi Bait and I mixed a can of C-ration boned chicken with an envelope of dehydrated chicken and noodle soup from the world. "Numah fucking one, GI."

We had the first two shifts of radio watch and stayed up together the whole time, talking and drinking C-ration hot chocolate.

We talked about what we would do when we got back. Fi Bait said he really didn't want to but would probably go to grad school for lack of anything better to do. Besides, it was almost a moral obligation to use that GI Bill, get something over on the army for once. You could just fuck off for a year and still draw it the whole time. I told him if I went back to school I would get sick every time I saw a motherfucking student. It would be great to just expatriate.

"How the fuck would you live?"

"I don't know. Be a fucking foreign service officer."

"Rather go to grad school and fuck some colonel's daughter, a freshman. You join the foreign service and they'll put you in the Saigon embassy."

We laughed, moving to other devious ways to get back at the world. It was always a good feeling to be in your hootch and talking, the rain beating on the stretched ponchos. If only you had dry clothes, but you got used to being wet, too.

We got up at five-thirty in the morning and followed the trail right into the village. There were banana and pineapple trees on the way in, Kell picked a bunch of bananas and we quietly passed them around. They were only half as big as those you got in the world, but sweeter.

You could hear the dogs yapping as we approached. Everyone was awake and standing before the houses, in a circle of dull brown thatched houses on stilts, completely surrounded by trees and jungle. One house had two walls made out of C-ration cases. The chief, or whatever you call him, was standing there smiling in front of the others to greet us.

Plei Jan was used to GIs passing through. It was known as a friendly village, that's why we could walk right in with just a platoon instead of spreading a cordon and searching house to house like on television.

None of the Montagnards spoke English, and none of us spoke whatever they speak—I don't know if they speak Vietnamese; they're racially different and are known to despise the Vietnamese as corrupt and cunning.

Montagnards are primitive, they live off the pineapples, I guess. Plei Jan had only one water buffalo in the whole village, and I didn't see any rice paddies or farm crops. There were a few pigs, brown with black stripes, and several ducks and chickens, besides the dogs.

The people were barefoot. The men reminded me of movie Indians with the rope and square of cloth hanging over ass and groin. The women had coarse black skirts and nothing above the waist. The breasts on even the girls drooped and flopped whenever they walked.

They all hovered behind the chief, old men and women grinning and gazing. Most Montagnard women smoke pipes. One shrivelled old doll had an American corn cob like Mammy Yokum. When she took it out and smiled the black toothless gums Fi Bait poked me in the side and we both laughed.

All the chief would do was grunt and smile, bowing his head and spreading his arm like someone showing you through the door. Lieutenant Chivington nodded back and muttered to him.

"Numah one, Papa-san. GI friend. We numah one."

He gave him two packages of chewing tobacco. Nobody chews it, so when the supplementary ration packages were opened we would save it for such uses. The chief giggled hysterically and pointed his pinched fingers to his mouth, nodding the head.

The lieutenant nodded to Kell, and the rifle squads began moving among the houses. Fi Bait, Phil, Fleming, and I stayed with the chief and lieutenant. We took our packs off and set the rifles on them.

Lieutenant Chivington unstrapped his ruck and pulled out a carton of licorice. When he threw the boxes on the ground all the naked kids squealed and scrambled for it like football players with a fumble.

But one kid who looked to be nine or ten stood silently beside the chief. He had the rope and Indian groin towel like the men and stared at me with an expressionless face. I could detect neither contempt nor curiosity; he just stood there gazing, piercing into me. I took the Milky Way I had been saving for lunch from my sandbag and pointed it to him. He took it with no response and stepped back, holding it at his side, his small black eyes shining like marbles.

"Wow man, what's with the fucking Milky Way?" asked the medic.

"I'm a softy," I said.

"I wouldn't give no Milky Ways to no Yards," said Lieutenant Chivington.

"You could have given it to me if you didn't want it, shitbird," said Fi Bait.

"Fuck it."

The chief opened a package of chewing tobacco and crammed two handfuls into his mouth. He muttered and giggled as he chewed.

Kell came back alone, strutting bowlegged.

"Didn't find nothin, sir."

"Okay. I ain't gonna fuck with sendin somebody down the well to check."

"What about the water buffalo pit?"

"Hell *no.* Unless you feel like goin in there yourself."

"Not today."

"Tell the men to go ahead and eat breakfast. Satank'll play doctor and we should be able to move out by ten o'clock."

"Roger."

Roger. Only a lifer would say roger. He strutted away with the short M-79 barrel on his shoulder, like a stateside soldier walking guard with a rifle.

"Lieutenant, do you court-martial guys for cookin with C-4?" asked Fi Bait.

"If you got some let me have a piece. Heat tabs are hard to come by."

The chief and his hovering kids stood there watching us as we sat on the ground and ate. The bastard with my Milky Way kept staring at me—with no expression, just like a statue. I threw my crackers at his feet. I don't know why, though I never ate crackers anyway. He picked them up and stayed at the chief's side. Naturally he didn't eat them, just held them in the same hand with the Milky Way.

Phil opened his medical bag after breakfast, and the chief went around yelling in the houses. From the rear he really did look like an old Indian, with the cloth over his ass and the long stringy white hair, spindly but straight legs. The women lined up before Phil with their naked babies just like in the commercials for UNICEF or Project Hope.

If the kids had cuts or sores Phil would wash them with peroxide and apply mercurochrome. He didn't check the women or old men unless they made a gesture. One old man had a cut knee, a pregnant girl some kind of eye infection. All he could do was wash the eye and try to tell her to keep washing it each day.

The rest of the patrol fraternized with the kids and old women as they came out of line. Big Sam convinced Mammy Yokum to let him smoke her pipe and everyone, GI and Montagnard, screamed laughing as he choked.

Phil was about through when Mastion appeared from the side of a house with his arm around a Montagnard girl, grin on his face.

Everybody gets horny, but my God.

I guess the girl wasn't bad for a Yard. Her face wasn't as greasy, the breasts didn't droop like an old woman's and the small black nipples were symmetrical. The bare feet reminded me of Kentucky. She had the traditional Montagnard gold rings in her ears and three bracelets on the right wrist. Dwarfed by Mastion, and with the same emotionless expression as the kid with my Milky Way and crackers.

The lieutenant saw him.

"You been fuckin, Mastion?"

All the grunts moaned, that long snickering moan like a first-grade class when someone is caught chewing gum.

"Sir, I wouldn't think of it."

He let the girl go and smiled big.

"It ain't funny, dick head. You know I could get you court-martialed for that?"

"I didn't do anything, lieutenant," brushing the red moustache with his third finger and snickering.

The girl went over to a huddle of old women and they all started yapping.

"You fucking asshole."

I think Lieutenant Chivington was really getting pissed off, but Phil was finishing with the last kid. Mastion ignored him and started talking with Taylor, a grunt from Pennsylvania. The lieutenant just eyeballed him and told us to police our trash and pack up. He was still eyeballing Mastion as Fleming gave him the handset.

"Raider eight-five this is Raider three-four, over," using the standard Hollywood call sign procedure.

"This is Raider eight-five."

"Roger, this is Raider three-four, have completed hamlet inspection, negative sit-rep. Am proceeding back to your location at this time, over."

"This is Raider eight-five, understand, negative sit-rep, you'll sierra papa at this time. How's my copy, over?"

"This is Raider three-four, good copy. Negative further, out."

Fleming hooked the handset back to his chest.

"Okay, let's move out."

Mastion clamped his shotgun closed and moved to the point, shotgun tucked under his arm and combing the red moustache with his other hand.

The chief giggled and waved.

Lieutenant Chivington waved back. "Numah one, Papasan."

Everyone else in the village stared quietly. The bastard with my Milky Way was still at the chief's side.

Plei Jan. Pacified village.

We had gone five hundred meters down the trail when the tubes popped. Three thups, three tubes. We all froze. Not more than five seconds and we heard the hollow rushing and rumbling. Looking back it was so much like a movie. It always was; as I reminisce, that's the most striking and revolting thing about it.

They came in as we were diving to the bush. Falling hollow rumbling, spit-second suction noise just before the explosion goes, a solid reverberating explosion, unlike C-4. Fleming was hit with that first volley and screamed, one short hoarse piercing scream, cut off.

Phil had thrown himself behind Fi Bait and me and ran to the other side of the trail to help Fleming just as the tubes popped again. This time six rounds, two per tube.

Fi Bait hit my shoulder, grabbed the handset and started yelling.

"Break break break, this is seven-three-seven, fire mission! All stations break."

"Send your grid seven-three-seven."

The rounds came in. I about shit, pressing both hands on the steel pot. One hit on the trail between us and Phil. I heard the shrapnel cut and whiz through the leaves around me. I was scared shitless. In a fire fight you're too busy shooting back to get scared. But you're helpless against mortars; all you can do is lie there and listen to the thups of the tubes and wait for the explosions and shrapnel. Helpless. That hollow tumbling rushing as they come in, suction as the explosion goes.

"Come up on grid 864-036. ASAP, we've got in-coming and WIAs."

"Roger, 864-036."

Fleming was quiet.

"Anybody else hit?" Phil screamed.

No answers. I looked over at him through the smoke. He was folding the poncho, standard field expediency for a sucking chest wound.

It was too quiet. Just like in the goddamned movies. Too quiet, staring across at Phil. Where was the next one going to hit? Sweating and panting. I wanted to run, do *something.*

"Seven-three-seven, that grid is a friendly village, over."

"They're fuckin mortarin us, you shit-bird!"

They popped again, muffled thups stopping the blood in my face. I gulped and tucked my chin deeper into my chest. Just lying there, knowing it was coming.

"God damn it, level the place!"

"That's a registered village, you idiot."

"They're bringin the max on us for Christ's sake!"

This time the dispersion was greater. All hit ahead of us and right of the trail. Maybe they figured we'd be running. Someone screamed from near the point.

"How bad?" yelled Phil.

"My fucking shoulder." It was Taylor, from Pennsylvania.

Phil ran up the trail clutching his medical bag. I saw him leap, running like a football back breaking through the line. He had jettisoned his ruck and rifle.

The acrid smoke floated through the bush and Fi Bait screamed again above the silence.

"God damn it they're killin us! Give me a battery six HE. Give me a goddamned arc light."

'This is red leg four-seven. That's a big negative. You know I can't fire on a friendly village without higher authorization, over."

"Kiss my ass motherfucker!"

"Seven-three-seven you use that kind of talk on this radio and you'll have an Article Fifteen waitin for you, boy."

"What the fuck's wrong with you?"

Fai Bait no longer screamed but was plaintive, face flushed, skin drawn tight around the eyes.

No more rounds came in. They probably figured we would be retaliating with artillery and had moved back out of the village. The whole thing couldn't have lasted over three minutes.

"This is red leg . . ."

Fi Bait keyed the handset so the voice couldn't come through.

"This is seven-three-seven, kiss my ass, lifer. Negative further, out."

At the time I was too stunned by the situation to think about it, but looking back that stands out as one of the most beautiful scenes of my life. "Kiss my ass, lifer." I wish I had said that to somebody at some time in my military career.

The silence was maddening, just like the fire fight, approaching panic. All you could do was lie there, waiting for something to happen. I watched a centipede crawl down a bamboo shoot. Finally Phil came running back down the trail to Fleming.

Fi Bait dropped the handset on the damp ground and pushed my head back down so he could turn the radio off. We got up and clustered around the medic with everyone else. I was till unable to swallow my Adam's apple, eyes dry and blinking.

Two grunts picked Fleming up and lay him on the trail. The poncho lay loose on his chest, over the dressing. Blood still trickled out in two streams on the left side, puddling on the yellow dirt just like in the movies. He had probably died before Phil had finished so he didn't bother completing the job. Fleming's mouth and eyes were closed. Just like in the goddamned movies—I guess in the movies it's close to half and half, half with the eyes open, the other half shut.

Another grunt carried Fleming's pack out. I had thought Fleming was the only guy hit, but Phil nodded to the bush and two other guys went in for Lieutenant Chivington. One piece of shrapnel had cut across his face and taken his right eyebrow completely off, blood glistening down the cheek to the throat. It was like Henry Cooper's eye when Cassius Clay got to him, only the cut was much deeper, probably all the way into the skull. The front of his shirt was completely red. We later learned from base camp that he had taken a total of nineteen pieces of shrapnel in the chest and head.

I don't know, fucked up world.

Lieutenant Chivington and Fleming were both KIAs. Phil left the poncho lying on Fleming's chest. He took off each man's boots and Kell called for a dust-off. Taylor was the only WIA, and it was only a scratch. One of the first volley's three rounds had gotten both the lieutenant and Fleming. They were evidently diving for the bush when it hit, because both had their chests chewed up.

Phil gave Kell the dog tags and tied a KIA tag to each man's left big toe. We lay their gear beside the bodies and sat waiting for the medevac. A few guys opened C-ration accessory envelopes and smoked the cigarettes.

Kell popped yellow smoke when the bird came in. It hovered so high that we didn't get any backwash, the rotors slapping almost like a sixty instead of the grinding and numbing roar. The crew chief swung the Penetrator's steel arm out and lowered the cable, big white square and red cross shining down at us.

Phil and Kell secured Fleming in the sling and the crew chief hauled him up, then sent it back down for Lieutenant Chivington; then again with a basket, for their rifles, boots, and packs. Swinging the arm back in he looked down at us and flashed the peace sign. Peace sign. I remember wanting to shoot him as I stared up at the curved plastic helmet visor over his face.

The bird hovered higher above the triple canopy before arching off. Nothing was said until the rotors' noise had faded.

"Okay, let's saddle up," said Kell.

He had taken the radio out of Fleming's pack and put it in his own while waiting for the bird. We slung the packs and huddled around him, above the pool of Fleming's blood.

"Raider eight-five this is Raider three-four, over."

"Send your traffic, three-four."

"Roger, this is three-four. Kilo-India-Alphas dusted off, am proceeding to your location at this time, over."

"Roger, three-four. Come on in, boy."

Kell hooked the handset to the metal ring on his ruck strap, Mastion took the point with his shotgun and we walked back toward Jude. Kell was now in charge of the first platoon.

We stopped at four o'clock and set up our november lima in a plain of elephant grass. I don't know why we didn't keep going until finding a bamboo grove as usual; we had to send five guys out to cut enough poles and stakes for everybody's hootches. It started raining before they got back and by the time we had the hootches up we were all soaked.

I had beef and shrapnel for supper; Fi Bait had spaghetti. We hadn't spoken to each other since leaving the village. The radio was still turned off.

"You gonna send in a november lima?"

"Fuck it," he said.

I didn't want to force conversation, but I also knew if he kept the radio off and didn't turn in a november lima his shit would be flapping with the lifers.

"Want me to call it in?"

"Fuck," shaking his head. "Yeah, go ahead."

I coded our location and three on-call targets and sent them in. They didn't give any hassle about Fi Bait's tone that morning.

He lay on his back with the damp poncho liner tucked under his chin. "Tell me it ain't a fucked up world, Henry."

"I can't believe it."

"Fucking army. Fucking gooks . . . friendly village."

It rained until eight o'clock. Kell came over as soon as it stopped and told us our shifts for radio watch. Fi Bait was already asleep, at least had his eyes closed. Kell gave us the last shift and told me to wake him.

I had trouble sleeping that night. I thought back to the first fire fight, how it now seemed like an obscene game of cowboys and Indians. Kill a dink, no sweat; the blood today had been human, *real.* I thought about it and sulked nearly all night.

But I was in the Nam, I told myself that I was having trouble going to sleep only because that was the first time. As they say, "If you've seen one you've seen 'em all." I told myself that that principle applied to Americans as well as dinks. Next time it would be natural—though still sad, of course. It's just a fucked up world. After that night you would lose no sleep over KIAs, just like after actually killing one you would lose no sleep over killing dinks—so you told yourself.

I woke up Fi Bait and then Kell. It was still dark as we ate breakfast. We moved out with the sun pink behind glistening gray clouds and made it back to Jude by four o'clock, in time for a hot supper.

Captain Ferris called us over to the CP before the chow bird came in and talked about how they never would have sent us in there if they had expected anything like that. Phil was being put in for a bronze star with V, and Kell was to be promoted to staff sergeant. In the morning the chaplain would fly out for a funeral service, and the colonel would come with him to talk to us. We were to shave before getting into the chow line.

Big Sam and the medic ate at the table with Fi Bait and me.

"Bronze star, shit," said Phil.

"No use bein bitter," said Sam. "At least you're gettin somethin from the army for a change."

"Gettin shit. Why don't they give me a three-day R&R?"

"You'd get the clap," said Fi Bait.

"Your mother'll be proud of a bronze star," said Sam.

The chow was hot dogs and sauerkraut with the usual quart of milk for every two men. That night it didn't rain and the four of us sat at the table talking until dark. Gazing away from each other to the Hollywood Cambodian sunset as the talk got to Lieutenant Chivington and Fleming. Chivington had volunteered for the Nam, Fleming was US and had come in-country with Phil. I never did really know him.

After dark Sam brought a new candle over, we went into our bunker and played spades.

CHAPTER SEVEN

In the morning First Sergeant Ballard ran an on-line police call with everybody on the fire base except the guys on bunker guard, just like at Fort Polk. With both the battalion commander and the chaplain coming you *had* to have a strak fire base. He stood on top of the CP and threatened to give an Article Fifteen to anybody he caught eating between that time and the colonel's departure. Technically an Article Fifteen can be issued only by the company commander, but if a ranking NCO suggests one is needed it is never questioned. Each of us—even Fi Bait and I, who usually escaped such harassment—had an empty sandbag and lined up at the wire.

"All right men, move out and get it *all.*"

The NCOs walked behind the line to inspect. Old Sergeant First Class Skinner of the 81 platoon stood back at the starting line, hands at his hips. SFC Skinner. He was in his forties, from Alabama, had been in both World War II and Korea, infantry all the way. There he was in RVN, supervising an infantry police call. Except for Captain Granger of Echo company he was the only lifer to get any respect—perhaps more properly pity—from the troops. And yet he was still known as "shit man" because he was fanatical in making sure his mortarmen burned shit until the ashes were white, would throw a shit-fit when they didn't.

When the loach buzzed in, a CP RTO ran halfway down to the pad yelling, "Pop smoke," and the first sergeant eyeballed the perimeter for one last check of the state of police. Captain Ferris came out of his CP strutting, with steel pot on head and CAR 15—a special James Bond modified M-16—in his hand.

Loach is vernacular for LOH, light observation helicopter. The loach is half as big as a slick, shaped like an egg, has just a pilot and two people besides him. It usually has no armament, though occasionally a Head Hunter team leader will have a mini-gun. Each battalion commander has his own personal loach and pilot on call from base camp for whenever he wants to fly. They buzz like a rubber band motor compared to the beating slicks and Cobras, not to mention the mighty shit hooks.

Smoke popped purple. Captain Ferris strode down the trail to greet them at the pad. He wore his pistol belt, jungle boots shined black. Ducking but still holding his head perpendicular to the ground as he eyeballed, saluted, and shook the colonel's hand. The colonel put his arm around Captain Ferris's waist, talking above the turbine's buzz as they walked up. The chaplain trailed behind with his canvas bag, the pilot cut his engine and stayed at the pad smoking and talking with the pad man. First Sergeant Ballard double-timed down to the gate and greeted them with his heels locked, saluted, and fell in behind the colonel.

Fi Bait and I were alone at our table and watched the ritual. The chaplain waved at us but we just eyeballed as he passed. I felt like giving him the finger.

When the captain and colonel emerged from the CP the first sergeant yelled for everybody but the bunker guards to form for the funeral services. Fi Bait had the excuse of monitoring our radio and stayed at the table.

"They got you too?" Phil asked as I sat down on the damp dirt next to him. I shrugged. I was actually curious, I had only seen military funerals in the movies. When everyone had settled the chaplain pulled the yellow plastic tape recorder from his bag.

"Good morning, men."

Colonel Fetterman and Captain Ferris stood behind him. He put the tape recorder on the ground, draped the black sash over his neck, and began. First thing was the national anthem on the plastic tape recorder, everyone rising and locking heels. I about shit right there.

". . . Men, as you all know, a lieutenant and his RTO form a team. The platoon leader is helpless to lead without his radio, he can't communicate, he could get lost and fail in his mission. Yesterday the first platoon lost its leadership-communications team . . ."

Phil poked me and I nodded, without turning my eyes from the chaplain. *Un*-real. Colonel Fetterman stood staring at his boots, hands behind his back. John Wayne.

"Lieutenant Chivington was RA, volunteered to come to Vietnam. I don't know what his motives were, what his politics were. I like to think he just wanted to do the finest service he could to his country. Fleming was US, but he too answered his country's call. They were both soldiers, and like soldiers they answered the call, they gave the ultimate sacrifice. Just as I know all of you would, without quibbling. They died proud. 'Yea though I walk through the valley of the shadow of death I will fear no evil . . .' "

I don't know, maybe some guys, a few still-faithful Baptists if there were any—maybe Kell—maybe some really did get solace from it. Maybe some guys would rest in peace knowing someone was saying that over their dusted-off body.

To cap it off he had everybody stand.

". . . won't you bow your heads with me now in a moment of silent prayer?"

The inevitable climax; "Taps" on the yellow plastic tape recorder while we were still in silent prayer. Fuck me.

At least they didn't have the rifles stuck into the ground with bayonets and the helmets drooped over the stocks, like in the movies. Maybe they would have, if there had been any bayonets around—nobody uses them over there.

After "Taps" Colonel Fetterman stepped forward.

"Men, sit back down. I've got a few things for you."

The chaplain took the scarf off and put the tape recorder back in his bag. The colonel watched him, waiting until he had smiled at us, and started back towards the pad before going on.

I guess Colonel Fetterman was as tall as John Wayne,

and had a flabby gut, like the real John Wayne. He also held his hands behind his back and rocked sideways as he spoke. Steel pot with "Regulars by God" embroidered on the camouflage cover.

"Men I want you to know that I sympathize for Lieutenant Chivington. Want you to know tomorrow they're movin a Mike Strike unit into that goddamned village. If there's dinks there they'll bring *smoke* on their asses."

He paused, eye-balling, perhaps expecting a response, and narrowing his eyeballs at the silence.

"You know Lieutenant Chivington was in charge of the first platoon. Now I'm not sayin this just because he got it, but the first platoon Bravo Company has consistently shown itself to be the best rifle platoon I've got. Sergeant Kell there is now Staff Sergeant Kell. Damned good man."

Pacing, looking at the ground. "We now know that the first platoon fucked up yesterday. Staff Sergeant Kell says there were no young men in that village. Lieutenant Chivington should have found out where all the young men were as soon as he walked in. He should have suspected something."

"But that's neither here nor there. It's too fucking late now . . ."

He went on to what a fine job we were all doing. He wanted to give us a pat on the back, let us know he appreciated it. The going might get tough, but we were proving we were *men.* We could go back home and be proud of the suffering we had gone through and the service we had given our country. We were Regulars, by God.

When he left, Captain Ferris escorted him to the loach, squatting again to hold his head up and salute under the rotors. First Sergeant Ballard told the first platoon to stay there, everybody else could go back to their bunkers. He had me go get Fi Bait, too.

"You gotta go, Fi Bait."

"Gotta shit."

"First sergeant said."

"Fuck a bunch of first sergeants. You get your fill of military funerals for awhile?"

"I reckon I did."

He signed off the radio and left it at the table.

Briefing. Captain Ferris began by lighting a cigar, and told us to smoke if we wanted to. Most guys did light up.

"First of all men, Lieutenant Chivington got a Bronze Star posthumous, for what it's worth. I don't know what bullshit they made up, but like the old man says, that's neither here nor there. I don't know, his mother should be proud." He paused, puffing on the cigar and pacing, then right-facing back at us.

"Okay. Staff Sergeant Kell is now in charge of your platoon. God knows when we'll get another lieutenant. You guys are gettin the honor of playin another New Action Army experiment. As of tomorrow you'll work with a squad of Mike Strikes and an ARVN interpreter. I don't know what the fuckin' point is, but that's neither here nor there. There's supposed to be a Green Beret flyin out with the gooks to brief you in the morning. You'll be doin straight recon in force, check points, and I've informed First Sergeant Ballard that whenever you're back on the LZ the first platoon won't pull no bunker guard and won't burn no shit. Staff Sergeant Kell's one of the best there is in the bush, you know that. You also know these fuckin Mike Strikes are supposed to know their shit. I know you'll do all right. Any questions?"

Sam raised his hand.

"Shoot, Silton."

"Sir, are we exempt from bunker guard tonight?"

"Roger that."

Phil spoke up without raising his hand. "Are they puttin us with gooks as an experiment or just because it's a bad mission and they want fewer American casualty figures?"

The captain eyeballed him and flicked ashes from his cigar.

"Why the fuck are you askin that kind of question, Satank? You think the army's out to kill GIs?"

"But you're not Higher, sir. You can't say. If you've got a squad of gooks it cuts down the proportion of American KIAs in the element and looks better on TV. Doesn't it, sir?"

He emphasized the "sir."

Everybody groaned, that first-grade-class groan.

"At ease God damn it!" yelled the first sergeant. The captain was blushing.

"Satank you know in Colonel Fetterman's army you'd never get away with that shit." Flicking ashes. "If you've got to be clever and cynical why don't you keep it to yourself? One of these days you're gonna force somebody to court-martial your ass. If you've got an attitude problem at least have the goddamned brains to keep it to yourself."

The fact was that Phil had the captain by the balls and knew it. He was not only a good medic but the only one the first platoon had. You can't send a platoon out without its medic. If threatened with an Article Fifteen, Phil could demand a court martial; even if he knew they'd convict his ass at a court martial, he knew Captain Ferris couldn't afford it because it would put the first platoon without a medic for a noncombat-inflicted reason. That would put the platoon out of action and in turn aggravate Colonel Fetterman, who would thereby be influenced in his final Officer Evaluation of Captain Ferris when he left the Nam.

With the sermon and the two pep talks I guess Hollywood might say I had experienced the full trinity of war, or something. Kill a dink, see an American killed, mourn for him with the colonel and chaplain before the plastic tape recorder. Anyway after Plei Jan things steadily got worse, unbelievably worse, but I can only tell that it was worse by looking back. I didn't notice then; I didn't really notice anything. Everyone was the same, I'm sure of it. Kill a dink. See a dead GI. Some may have regained their premises after returning, but while you're there, everything blurs and is natural. Even that sermon.

CHAPTER EIGHT

I don't know if the blood-stripe promotion qualified Kell as a full-fledged lifer or not. After all, he was still only nineteen. Rank made in the Big V isn't like in the states. Over there it's given to fill an empty slot or in recognition of ability—with Kell it was a combination of both. In the states you made rank by playing soldier for X years and signing away X more years of your life. "Re-up." When you see a staff sergeant in the stateside army, there's no question he's a lifer.

Kell's attitude changed very little one way or another after Plei Jan. He didn't stop playing army, but he didn't become any more of a drill sergeant and didn't go out of his way to remind you that he was boss. He was naturally shy anyway—Kentucky—and I think the rank may have given him deeper humility. In his Hollywood perspective he probably saw himself as our leader and felt special obligations. Staff Sergeant Kell. Harlan County. I don't know, fucked up world.

They really did send a Green Beret out the day after the funeral. He and the ARVN interpreter came in on a loach and as soon as it lifted off a slick came in with the Mike Strikes. Mike Strikes are Montagnard and Cambodian mercenaries, recruited and trained by the Green Berets and having no direct relations with the Vietnamese army. For that reason I don't guess you should call them gooks. The ones with us were all Cambodians. They certainly were more human than the gooks.

The Green Beret was a captain, with a .38 revolver and

black leather holster. He carried a CAR-15 and no ruck sack. The interpreter and the Cambodians all carried M-16s and full gear, like us. They're all little people, gooks, dinks, Yards, and Cambodians alike, none of them over five feet. In their skin-tight, "tiger" fatigues—so named because of green and black waved stripes like a tiger's body—they looked even more frail. Yet they carried as much on their backs as we did. It's really surprising that they were never blown over by the backwash when we CA'd.

First Sergeant Ballard yelled for the first platoon and FO party to form by the CP. We stood in a semicircle around the Green Beret and his ARVN, the Mikes mixed in with us. They would smile at us as he talked. Not the calculated, humble gook-smile, but an honest, human smile, you could sense it. Right then I began to see them as comrades. Fellow fighting men, plus the reputation all Mikes had as ass-kickers. Skin-tight tiger fatigues and berets instead of steel pots.

It turned out that we were to CA that very afternoon. The Beret never did say why we were going with Mikes. We were to be inserted north of Plei Jan and recon along the river. He didn't know how long we would be out. We would be resupplied in the bush every four days until the mission was over.

Fuck me, mission. Maybe they expected us to make immediate contact, and if we didn't, keep us out until we did. I still don't know why they put us with Mikes, why they inserted us way up there. You could argue, like Phil, that it was to produce a lower percentage of American casualties, but that would be too rational. Maybe it was a sociological experiment to see how we would get along with Asians. Or maybe it was Hollywood, American-Asiatic cooperation at the grass roots; maybe they even planned on bringing in a journalist if all went well. I don't know.

After his briefing the Green Beret asked if there were any questions. I remember he wore the dark helicopter sunglasses and a real green beret, pacing as he talked.

No questions. No one had planned on going out that very day. I was especially apprehensive. The bizarre atmosphere of the whole thing, the very day after Lieutenant Chivington's funeral and the colonel's speech. A real Green Beret in the flesh, the notorious Mikes, my first CA, staying out in the jungle for perhaps an indefinite period. Fuck me.

At Fort Polk they always made the term CA particularly horrendous. And indeed, the real thing turns out to be even more so. Those last few seconds as the bird banks and circles in, with the gunship escorts below pounding rockets into the bush. Hovering four feet above the landing zone with the nose poised upward, anxious to get rid of you and make its departure. As the gunships begin working out you know it's coming and put your feet on the skid. Your emotions suspended in nausea as you float down, just waiting to see the guy next to you drop his weapon and start bleeding—that's the only way you know they're there, you can't hear rifles over the whine and pounding of the turbine and rotors.

After the Green Beret left in his loach, the ARVN and Mikes leaned against the CP smoking. First Sergeant Ballard told us to draw rations after lunch and assemble at the pad at 13:30 for the CA.

"We ain't gonna go today," said Fi Bait as we walked away.

"How do you know that?"

"By the time birds get here we'll be smacked in."

"Hope you're right."

My spirit rose, the fog was moving in from Cambodia.

It would only take ten minutes to pack, all we had to do was make the bed rolls and packs Cs, so Fi Bait and I spent the rest of the morning writing letters. I wrote my parents, a history professor, and the preacher. Fucking preacher.

Fi Bait wrote twelve pages to the French bitch.

His French bitch really was outstanding. In the picture she was in a red bikini, long black hair swung in front over the left shoulder and shining with the contour of the breast. She was leaning against a light pole at the beach, hands behind her back, those long legs, smiling big.

He would show me all her letters. She always signed,

"Amour, ta pauvre Française, Jeanne." I don't know if she really would give a blow job, but if she *would*. . .

She knew she'd never see him, it didn't matter what she said. Maybe the picture wasn't even her, probably wasn't.

I'm sure Fi Bait didn't really take the shit seriously either, it was just a good pastime. My God though, what a fuck. Those long firm legs.

Fi Bait spoke French but would always have me proofread his letters and translate words in hers that he didn't understand. She said she was a secretary, and wrote romantic letters that described the parks of Paris and the moon-lit sand of the Riviera, places for l'amour, even making the weather horny. Those long legs, those breasts. My God.

I had spaghetti for lunch and Fi Bait had beef and shrapnel. He asked for a classy ending to the letter, I told him, "Ton soldat triste, qui veut battre seulement pour tes seins belles."

"Holy fuck, I couldn't have done better, Mr. Winsted."

Fi Bait got a new map from the CP and we sent in on-call targets for the landing zone before packing. We were to be inserted in the flat marsh at a bend in the river, so all birds could go in at once.

I asked Fi Bait what a CA was like, blushing as I did, like a kid asking his father if the dentist really is that bad. He said to jump when he did and follow him. He would be following everybody else, unless it was a hot LZ, in which case just lie down and shoot until somebody figures out what's going on and what to do.

We were still sitting at the pad at two o'clock. The fog was there, but it hadn't set in, you could still see the valley floor.

"No birds today, GI," said Phil.

"No boondocks tonight," said Sam.

Everyone except the Mikes and Sam and me sat on the ground, backs against the stuffed rucks. The Mikes stood in a huddle at the concertina, rifles leaning against their thighs and all smoking. Sam and I stood talking by the water trailer. He kept his arms folded, moving his knees as he talked.

"Sit down, Henry," yelled Fi Bait. "You're makin me a nervous wreck."

"Sit the fuck down, shit-bird," said Phil.

"How am I supposed to act, Big Sam?"

Sam was over six feet tall, silhouetted against the white mist. The olive drab towel draped over his neck and the .45 low on his hip, stretching the jungle shirt tight on his perfectly flat chest. He had written "God is my point man" across the front of his camouflage cover. In red ink, just like Kell had put E-5 stripes on his.

"You know you won't miss the bird, Sam-bo. I'll personally save you a seat," said Jacobs.

Jacobs was a brother too, short and dumpy. He would always talk slow and in a serious tone, groaning the words.

"Sam-bo." Everyone ooh-ed, like in the first grade when someone is naughty. Jacobs lay on the ground with his head propped against the ruck, his sixteen on one side and the big sixty with bipods on the other.

"Kiss my ass," said Sam. "I'm standin, by God."

"Steadfast and Loyal," I said.

"Sit the fuck down," said Phil.

We shrugged to each other and sat down.

"Hey pad man, what's the fuckin hold-up on the birds?" yelled Kell.

"The problem is, Staff Sergeant, that they ain't here yet."

Everyone laughed. You could hear the ARVN behind us giggling and translating for the Mikes.

"What's the fuckin hold-up?"

"How the fuck am I supposed to know? They're military helicopters, ain't they?"

The rain finally started at three o'clock. Everyone started bitching. "Let's go back to the fuckin bunkers; we're gettin motherfuckin soaked for nothin." But all remained seated in the mud. As you sat there you could feel the rivulets form in the ground and flow into the seat of your pants. It was cold, but nobody went through the hassle of getting up or taking out a poncho. The Mikes kept in their huddle smoking.

Kell finally called the CP at three-thirty; they told him to stay there until they got an official cancellation.

"Mother-*fuck*," screamed Mastion. "Mother-*fuck* this goddamned army."

The rain had made his red mustache thin and longer, almost oriental. Water dripped from everyone's steel pots.

At four o'clock they finally called it off. Kell yelled up to the interpreter and everyone moved out, Mikes leading the way. One slipped in the mud and rolled into the concertina. The others pointed and giggled. He picked up his sixteen as he rolled back, getting up from all fours.

That night Fi Bait and I split a can of pudding I had left from a care package and smoked his A & C grenadiers. Our clothes had almost dried out on our bodies.

The Mikes had put up poncho hootches between the cramped sleeping bunkers, using engineer stakes for poles and split wood from 81 boxes for stakes. I went out to piss and would have pissed right on top of one if I hadn't heard them inside and then looked down and seen the ponchos. At night during monsoon it is pitch black because of the mist and clouds, no moon ever.

We were still smacked in next morning so they didn't bother to send us to the pad. However, by ten it had stopped raining and the fog was lifting.

First Sergeant Ballard came around screaming, "First platoon, saddle up and move down. First platoon . . ."

The ARVN rallied his Mikes and by eleven we were all back at the pad, like the day before, only today we sat on the packs instead of the mud. It wasn't raining and we might be able to stay dry, no use sitting in the mud. The Mikes again huddled at the gate.

I was halfway expecting another cancellation, but we hadn't been there ten minutes when the pad man got his call on the radio.

"Okay you guys, got four slicks on their way in."

My heart immediately throbbed. I gulped and jerked my pack up, holding my rifle between my legs. I was as apprehensive as after the fire fight and when we were mortared, although that hadn't been really apprehension but total fear.

It seems like CAs were the most abundant of all the television narratives, probably because they're so dramatic, the birds coming down in line and everyone jumping out. I think there was one commercial for savings bonds or something that showed a company-sized CA into a rice paddy.

The Cobras came in first and dove over the perimeter, as they had down at Clarissa. After two passes they circled high over the valley and the slicks came in. Four of them. Fi Bait and I stood leaning into the shrill backwash as the first bird sat down and men scrambled in from both sides. Phil was the last man in, he flashed the peace sign at us, legs dangling over the side. The door gunner too flashed the V, leaning out as the turbine slid back to the whine and slapping and they banked down to the valley. Then the pad man took his position like a football ref to guide the next bird in.

Fi Bait and I got in that second bird. He hit me on the back and we ran together into the backwash. I didn't want to sit with my legs dangling but had no choice, the middle of the bird was already filled. Actually it's best to sit on the edge, you can jump with no trouble—though I guess you're also a target on the way in.

We circled Jude with the Cobras while the other two birds loaded. It was like a carnival ride, I was facing down at the LZ holding my breath. I'm sure the guys on the other side could see nothing but clouds even if they looked down. Fi Bait nudged me, seeing that I was nervous. They say you can't fall out unless you're pushed, but I didn't need a demonstration.

Before leaving we all buzzed the LZ, first the gunships and then the slicks. Coming out of it we cut straight up, like Flash Gordon taking off. You could feel yourself being pushed back sideways.

The fog had dissipated and we followed high above the river. At high altitude it always seemed as if we were floating along the ridges and hills, the noise a gentle hum, like that very first ride from Clarissa to Jude. The Cobra on our side would keep slowing and dropping back, shooting past us up to the first slick, then dipping back again.

Fi Bait pointed down at Plei Jan. It was small but distinct through the triple canopy, the yellow flag with its red stripes pegged down or sewn to the roof of one of the houses so it wouldn't be shot at for target practice. As we passed the village the Cobra dropped below us, Fi Bait put a magazine in his rifle and pointed for me to do the same.

You could hear the first rockets shrieking even above the slick's noise, then the mini-guns and I saw the Cobra bank up and behind us to get in position for another dive. Our elevation dropped, you could see the terrain stop floating and begin whizzing by.

I gulped, this was it. The rockets shrieking. I told myself thank God it wouldn't last over a few minutes.

We went into a field of elephant grass at the bend in the river. The rockets were slamming in as our slick slowed and hovered, I saw the grass spread back in waves from the rotors, and Fi Bait hit me on the back to jump. I slid forward and touched the skid with both feet before going, everyone pushing around me and already running when I finally dropped. With the radio on my back I went flat on my chest, the wind knocked out of me. I lay there, the noise of the helicopters deafening, our bird zooming over my head and the next one already hovering, Cobra rockets shrieking and mini-guns ripping, backwash waving the grass around me with the grinding and whining noise. What was going on? Were there dinks? Was I the only one lying down?

I guess I would have kept lying there and perhaps panicked but Fi Bait, I don't know where he came from, hit my arm with his rifle and I pushed myself up. We ran for the tree line, about fifty feet ahead. I glanced around and Mikes were running with us. Kell was standing at the edge waving everyone in and counting them.

It turned out to be a cold LZ. We were all there. The slicks circled a few hundred feet ahead, Cobras kept expending on both sides of us. Fi Bait took my handset and told them we were safely inserted.

We stayed at the wood line and watched until the show

was over. The Cobras lanced out of the last dive, slicks converged to a straight line and the Cobras moved up and flanked the second bird. We watched them fade, trained mosquitoes, flitting and buzzing back to Pleiku.

CHAPTER NINE

This time Mastion carried a rifle. The Mikes would be our point squad. That first day was like any other patrol. We were breaking the bush and staying away from trails, and it was the same triple canopy as every place else. The river twisted and we crossed once, but it was only twenty feet wide, swift and no deeper than my waist; no one thought about leeches.

The Mikes are outstanding in the bush. They can shoot an azimuth and follow it, unlike many American point men, who lose the direction as soon as they have to detour an obstacle. Mikes can also read a map and know all the signs of dinks. Not that we didn't, I guess they were just more impressive—they *looked* like professionals, in the skin-tight tiger fatigues, Asiatics in their natural domain, the stalking hunters in pursuit of prey.

At lunch they would pull out plastic bags of rice instead of C-rations. When finished eating they always tied a knot in the bag, saving what was left for supper.

Phil offered one a few spoonfuls of beans and meatballs in exchange for a sample of rice the first afternoon. He said it was all right but needed sugar. I think his gesture impressed the Mikes, they all smiled and watched him eat.

"How many days, sarge?" Fi Bait asked Kell before we moved out again.

"Six-niner."

"Wow, how would you act?" asked Sam.

"Horny, brother," said Jacobs, dusting the sixty's feed tray with a toothbrush.

Kell was the shortest man there. Next in line were Mastion and Fi Bait, though Fi Bait had over four months to go.

We covered three check points that day. It was rough humping, ridges and triple canopy, but the Mikes were breaking bush and moving slow so it didn't kick my ass as bad as most Jude patrols. I had learned to live with it anyway.

At each check point we would take a break and let the Mikes recon the area. We made our november lima at check point three, a ridge directly above a rapids. It didn't rain until after dark, Fi Bait and I had just finished eating when we heard the Mikes giggling. He crawled out to see what was going on and told me to come out.

They were sitting in a circle, with Phil doing magic tricks. They squealed when he pulled the monkey pod out of one Mike's ear, another's collar. One of them excitedly motioned that he wanted to try it, but when Phil gave him the nut all he could do was hold it and scratch his head. The others pointed and laughed hysterically.

Kell heard it and joined the party, standing by me with his arms folded. He too giggled. Smiling wide and unpretentiously, the flat jaw jutting forward and the Kentucky Adam's apple vibrating; as innocent as one of the Mikes.

But soon the giggling had drawn half the platoon around the circle and Kell had to break it up. Said it was too much noise and one mortar round would get us all.

That night you could hear the rapids gushing behind the rain. I went to sleep thinking of Kentucky, probably because of Kell. My grandpaw with his sparse gray whiskers and "chaw tobaccer" in his gums. George Main waving from his new John Deere tractor as I walked up Dry Branch with my basket of packaged seed. I would wave back, scratching a poplar switch through the yellow dirt, moving barefoot up Dry Branch with Sally the old beagle bitch prancing at my side.

It was still raining in the morning and didn't stop all day. We covered three more check points. No signs of dinks. Rain again all that night, and again the third day, and by then you could feel the unease, like in a damned movie. We could be out there *forever* before the lifers brought us in. Going to sleep soaked in mud, waking up soaked again. Before long no one even talked, not even Sam and Fi Bait, who were generally the two loosest guys.

At lunch or on a break we would just sit there in the rain, quiet. I remember Mastion especially. He was always a loner anyway, except when he was blowing joints. Every day his face grew more emotionless, reminding me of that kid at Plei Jan who had my Milky Way. We were all getting growths of stubble beard, and the red glistened on Mastion's face.

The fourth day it cleared, Higher called in that morning and said we would be resupplied at 14:00 at check point two. We reached check point two at ten o'clock and sat in a perimeter to relax until the bird came.

We pulled off our boots and shirts and basked in the sun, Phil started fraternizing with the Mikes and we talked again. Phil asked Fi Bait to show the Mikes the French bitch but he didn't have the picture. Phil moved his hands in the shape of a woman's figure and the Mikes poked each other and giggled.

Kell took three guys and cut a small drop zone from a bamboo clump directly behind Fi Bait and me. I was down to a can of cheese and crackers, Phil ate ham and eggs and Fi Bait had nothing left. We were looking forward to getting more Cs.

When they finally called on the radio, the bird was already beating in. Mastion popped smoke and stood in the drop zone. It hovered fifteen feet off the ground, I was close enough to get stung by the swirling stones and dirt and grabbed my shirt as the door gunners started kicking the C-rations out. I had my head tucked under the shirt, and when Fi Bait slugged me in the back I whirled on him—which he of course wanted me to do. He had the handset and pointed to the drop zone. I saw Mastion in the prone, the bird leaving. Everyone was opening up. I grabbed my rifle and started shooting by instinct, not aiming at anything, not yet fully comprehending. Kell and Fi Bait lay beside me screaming into their radios.

With the bird's rotors still discernible, Silton and Jacobs

dove between Fi Bait and me, squeezing me aside. When everyone finally stopped Kell yelled to check fire and Sam started spraying with short bursts. Big Sam and his sixty, with Jacobs lying low at his side and the barrel blazing. Both their naked backs glistened with sweat, bamboo slivers and dirt standing out as on glistening wet paint.

By then I knew it had been a sniper. Sam was reconning by fire, random bursts of five or six rounds trying to either hit something or draw return fire. Kell told Fi Bait "No artillery" and yelled for the ARVN. The gook low-crawled and Kell told him to send four Mikes out to see if they could find a trail.

As soon as Sam stopped the Mikes took off running, dashing out of the perimeter and yelling commands to each other, zig-zagging over the C-ration cases. When they came back the ARVN said they had found one trail, but that was all. Kell called in the sit-rep to Higher.

We all knew what it meant. They had been *waiting* for that bird, we were being watched and followed. We could be ambushed or picked off individually at the dink's leisure.

Kell kept his cool, like a leader. When the Mikes returned he told us to break down the rations and be sure to open and stomp anything we didn't want so the dinks couldn't get it. We put our shirts and boots back on and checked our rifles and rucks. When the Cs were packed we moved out as if nothing had happened. But we all knew what was going on.

You can never forget the feeling. You can forget none of the pitifully Hollywood feelings, and they're all unique. The total fear and helplessness right after the fire fight is worst of all. The thing with a sniper is the inescapable anticipation as you walk, knowing he's there, he could shoot at any second, at any target; the tension, knowing instinctively that he was aiming at you personally. You could subdue it, I forced myself to conjure the Ultimate Woman, but you couldn't get it out of your mind. Maybe marijuana could, I don't know, but nobody ever used it until night. I never did at all.

Fortunately, the dinks were strategists. They would

only shoot at a valuable target, like a bird. Their intelligence purposes were served just by trailing us. If we got too close to a bunker complex they could stage an L-shaped ambush and annihilate us. Otherwise it was senseless to waste a sniper's bullet on some grunts. The only worthwhile target was a bird, unless they wanted to play with your mind by shooting a GI once a day. But they only did that when large elements were moving in a search and destroy. This time they were probably just interested in seeing where we were headed and took the bird as a target of opportunity. They did not open up again until the next resupply, at which time they were again waiting at the edge of the drop zone.

But of course even that explanation of dink strategy didn't comfort us. Everyone brooded, even the Mikes. It also rained that afternoon.

From then on whenever we stopped we would form a tight perimeter and half of us would lie prone, watching the wood line with weapons off safety, while the other half shit, pissed, or whatever. The same thing when we set up our november lima, only half of us worked while the others watched the jungle.

The morning after that first resupply they called and told us we were to recon a hill that had formerly been an American LZ. We would be extracted from there and flown back to Jude, end of mission.

They gave us a new set of check points to cover on the route of march, so we would be out five more days.

Maybe this definite goal, knowing you only had five days to go, then only fourteen meals, then only three days and a wake-up; maybe being able to divide and calculate the time eased the tension for some. But the tension was still there. Why were we way up there, why where we with fucking Mikes? Why were the dinks following us?

After three more days and three nights without incident perhaps some guys were feeling better, but then the second resupply bird drew sniper fire. We had cut a drop zone in the morning, as before, and this time the bird drew fire as soon as it hovered. The door gunners only kicked out three cases of Cs and took off. Again no one was hit, not even the door gunners; again we reconned by fire and sent four Mikes on their trail. When they returned the leader smiled and shook his head, squatting in conference with Kell and the ARVN.

"Okay, let's divide up Cs and saddle up."

"Saddle up, *shit*," screamed Mastion. Just like that. He was lying in the perimeter beside a Mike, straining his neck to look back at Kell and the steel pot pushed back above his hair line.

"Where the *fuck* are we goin?"

"Knock it off, God damn it," said Kell. Kell was beside Fi Bait. I had to twist my neck to see Mastion opposite us in the circle.

"You motherfucking lifer!"

Phil hit Mastion on the shoulder. "Hey, God damn it."

You could feel the violence coming as Mastion eyeballed Phil, lying there with his red whiskers and mustache glistening. But he didn't retaliate.

"That motherfucker's gonna get us all killed, doc."

Kell was blushing. I remember the swollen Adam's apple, stretching the skin of his neck. That flat jutting jaw.

"What the fuck could you do that he ain't doin?" asked Fi Bait, in a strained whisper. Fi Bait and the medic recognized a crisis and deliberately worked as a team. The Mikes started mumbling.

"Fuck," said Mastion.

He just shook his head, and Kell saw his opening.

"I don't want my shit blown away any more than anybody, Mastion. We're here, what the fuck can I do? You wanna take over? You want my stripes?"

That was pushing too far, *too* Hollywood. It's one thing to keep leadership to prevent panic but another to rub it in. Especially a guy with the lifer image that Kell had.

Mastion screamed, "You sorry fucker!"

I think he would have leaped and gotten violent if Phil hadn't grabbed him again.

"Mastion," a frantic half-whisper, just like in the movies when the sidekick keeps the keyed-up hero from doing something he would later regret.

Mastion eyeballed Kell and finally turned his head back pushing Phil's hand away.

"Okay, let's break out them Cs," Kell said.

Silton nudged me and nodded to the drop zone. I got up and went to get two cases—I don't know why, I could have been *shot*. Jacobs followed me out for the other case.

We only got two meals per man on the average, but that should have done us since we would move out for the hill in the morning and be back on Jude that night.

It didn't rain, but that didn't lift anybody's spirits. The dinks were watching, and there must be something on that hill or they wouldn't have sent us out there. That night I pictured myself charging up the hill with machine gun bullets ricocheting at my feet, dinks in sight with their machine guns blazing as we charged.

We set up our november lima at the last check point, which was right at the base of the hill. Everyone *knew* we were in for bad shit. You just knew it. Like in a goddamned movie. No one spoke. No one showed any emotion as we ate the cold Cs. Kell said no cooking, they would smell or see the flame and know it was a good time for a bushwack.

We were set up for two hours before dark. Sam came over and tried to force light-hearted conversation about the French bitch. We talked about her but didn't laugh. It was suddenly obscene. Sam sitting there at the foot of Fi Bait's air mattress.

"Want to see me blow Bubblegum Bob's mind?" asked Fi Bait. Bubblegum Bob was the name we had given to one of the RTOs at artillery liaison. Whenever he talked on the radio it sounded like he had a mouthful of bubblegum.

"Fuck Bob."

"Go ahead Fi Bait and blow his fuckin mind," said Sam.

"Red leg three-zero this is blue leg six-niner, over."

"Six-niner, this is three-zero Bravo, send your traffic boy."

It was Bubblegum Bob himself.

"Roger, my four-seven would like a sit-rep on romeo sierra for the colonials with our element, over."

"Colonials?"

"This is blue leg six-niner, that's most affirm. Would like sit-rep on romeo sierra, over."

"Roger, wait one, I have to check with three-zero Alpha."

"Standing by."

"Roger, six-niner, this is three-zero Bravo. Is that a code word?"

"This is blue leg six-niner, cannot transmit in clear, over."

"Roger, understand. This is three-zero Bravo, we have no record of colonials here. Must be top secret."

Fi Bait glanced at me and looked down, deciding to quit forcing it.

"Roger, this is blue leg six-niner, due to nature of mission I cannot discuss."

"Roger, wilco, six-niner, good luck buddy. Out."

Ever since the first sniper we had made our november lima especially tight, so that everyone could quickly communicate and the dinks would be less apt to sneak up close enough to throw a satchel charge. That last night before we approached the hill I could smell the acrid marijuana even before dark.

"Js?" I asked.

"Yeah," said Sam. He glanced out the hootch. "From the Mikes' side."

"I don't blame 'em," said Fi Bait.

It was almost dark when Sam left. The thin clouds were probably purpling and the sun red behind them, but you couldn't see through the triple canopy.

Sam was standing in front of our hootch when the scene began with Kell and the ARVN. We could hear them even inside.

"Pot okay."

"Whattaya mean, okay? How they gonna pull guard if they're high?"

"Okay," said the ARVN, "Okay."

"Okay, shit! You tell 'em to put 'em out."

Sam told us to come out and watch.

"Is okay, staff sergeant. Don't mean nothing, no sweat."

The ARVN was smiling and nodding at Kell. He patted his shoulder; I'm sure he was high.

He had both hands stretched on Kell's shoulders when Mastion crawled out of one of the Mikes' hootches.

"Is okay. No sweat," said Mastion in a forced, deep voice. He stood there smiling, with his arms folded like an Indian.

The Mikes crawled out after him. Two had joints in their hands.

"What the fuck are you doin, Mastion?" speaking in the half-whisper.

"Me do nothing, drill sergeant," in a deep voice like an Indian.

"I'm gonna turn your ass in, Mastion. This is it."

"No sweat," said the smiling ARVN.

Kell shoved him away.

"No push him, drill sergeant," said Mastion. Everyone was watching, though all but Fi Bait, Sam, and I were in their hootches looking out. The three of us knelt by our hootch. Kell and Mastion and the Mikes stood right up in the perimeter.

"What the fuck's wrong with you, Mastion?"

"What's wrong with you, drill sergeant? Why can't you leave people alone? You wanna play your soldier game, leave us alone, leave us *out.*"

He talked loud and put his arm around one of the smiling Mikes. "Why don't you have us shot at sunrise?"

Kell turned back to the ARVN, who immediately smiled, "No *sweat*, staff sergeant." In that soft childlike gook voice. Mastion's red mustache and whiskers glistened with sweat.

"You'll get it, Mastion." He turned to walk away but stopped when he saw everyone else was watching. He looked around. The condemned but innocent rustler eyeballing the mob for one compassionate face before they hung him. He had been shut down again.

Kell walked to his hootch with head low, Phil lying on his chest and eyeballing as he crawled in. The short, bow-legged strides, flat jaw and the Kentucky Adam's apple. Poor bastard.

We waited until eight o'clock in the morning before moving out, so that artillery and gunships would respond quicker; any earlier and the artillery would have most of their men sleeping, as would gunships back at Pleiku. On the map the peak was four hundred meters above our november lima. We would be going up the most gradual slope. If anything was there, we would creep back down without engaging them and call in the sit-rep to Higher, who would decide what to do; probably an artillery barrage and napalm.

No one spoke during breakfast, and we sat around for nearly an hour, packs and weapons ready to go. Fi Bait and I worked up several on-call targets to our flanks and called them in. Another RTO answered and didn't give us any hassle about Bubblegum Bob and the colonials.

Finally Kell stood up and squashed his cigarette with his heel.

"Okay, let's saddle up."

As we stirred he called Higher. Everyone saw Mastion walk over to him, stopped and stared.

"I ain't goin up that goddamned hill."

Kell blushed. Mastion was standing directly in front of him with arms folded, red whiskers glistening, yet, looking back, I think his tone was more of self-pity than defiance.

"The hell you ain't."

"There's no way, Kell. Fuckin dinks are waitin for us." He was almost pleading. I think Kell saw it.

"So you're gonna stay here by yourself?"

Kell was cool, not blushing as he looked up at Mastion, also out of character.

"I said I ain't goin, lifer."

"Look Mastion, your shit's in the fan already. Don't push it, boy."

Boy.

Everyone else had their rucks on but stood watching.

"You fucking lifer. What's wrong with you? You don't have to go up there. Call 'em up and tell 'em there's nothin there."

"What would happen if everybody felt that way?"

"We wouldn't *be* here, you fucking asshole."

If someone had backed Mastion up, we may have had a real Hollywood mutiny, but everyone just eyeballed. They've got you by the balls, unless the man in charge feels the same way, and even if he did he couldn't be sure but what some potential lifer in the platoon wouldn't turn everyone in.

"Look Mastion, we've got a mission, and we're gonna carry it out."

"Mission!" Mastion threw his hands up. "Mission!"

He wasn't yelling, more like pleading. He was still too levelheaded to break that jungle code of silence.

"I can't take it. I can't fucking take it."

"All we're gonna do is recon the hill. There's nothin there. If they thought we were gonna get our ass kicked they wouldn't have sent us out here."

"Wouldn't have sent us out here." He turned to the men, spreading his arms like Jesus. "Fi Bait, Phil, tell him, will you? You *know* there's dinks up there. You gonna follow him up there and get your shit blown away?"

I'm glad he didn't call my name. Actually, I don't know if Mastion ever knew my name. We never spoke.

"You better knock it off, Mastion."

Mastion just shook his head.

"I can't take it."

I think Kell must have noticed the new fatalism. Before he had always backed away from Mastion. He would never talk down at him that way, would never call him "boy."

"We're goin up that hill, Mastion, and you're goin too. If the gooks weren't with us you'd walk *point*."

"Wow." Mastion's voice faltered, shaking his head. "Wow, man. Yes, yes, drill sergeant. I'm goin up your motherfuckin hill. I'm gonna play your fuckin game."

He walked back and jerked the ruck to his shoulders. Kell called on the radio and told them we were on our way.

"Someday some GI's gonna *kill* you, you goddamned lifer. Fucking mission. You . . ."

His eyes were actually glistening. If he had shot Kell I would have sympathized. Everyone else was like me; they couldn't afford any hassle. But Mastion shouldn't have cared about the hassle. If he really wanted to rebel, then he should have gone all the way, not just to the point of self-pity and marijuana. Sometimes you like to think that that morning he came close to making the decision. The caged human, trying to muster one last bit of character, to *fight;* you sat there on the edge of your seat in the audience, hoping that he would do it, that he would come through, *kill* the lifer.

But he didn't. Fatalism. He picked up his sixteen and raised it over his head like an Indian on his horse; but that was all, he didn't go through with it.

"You've had it, motherfucker," said Kell. He pointed at the ARVN, "Tell your men to move out."

The ARVN muttered to the Mikes, who had already saddled up and had watched the show like us. Each chambered a round and they moved out at five meter intervals. I hunched my shoulders under the pack and fell in behind Fi Bait.

The point man was so far ahead that I could hear his machete only when he accidentally hit a branch at the wrong angle, making a crack. We walked for twenty minutes and were two-thirds of the way up when they opened up.

A lifer might call it a textbook ambush. To get out we would have to either charge up the hill, which meant annihilation from the AKs, or hit the prone and fight, in which case they would crawl in too close for us to call in artillery without calling it on ourselves. The only other option would be to run down the hill, and the machine gun was waiting for us.

They naturally let us walk past the machine gun. The AKs opened up from the left, that paralyzing popcorn popping. We hit the prone and returned fire, in an extended straight line spaced in the five meter intervals instead of a perimeter. Fi Bait screamed on the radio. I couldn't see a distinct target because of the bush, which also prevented them from getting a clear target as long as we were prone.

After we stopped the first volley I heard two wounded Mikes or dinks screaming above us, no way to tell which. The Mikes were taking the brunt of it, and in the interlude you could hear the bush rustle and the dinks shouting commands above us—harsh, cackling voices. Yet we didn't fire. I don't know why. A long, frustrating pause, almost as if each one, dink, GI, and Mike alike were waiting for the other. I'm sure the dinks were shifting position to form an arch above us and force us to retreat into the machine gun, which we still didn't know was there. They would probably get behind trees so their own machine gun wouldn't hit them.

"Let's move up!" screamed Kell.

No one moved. He looked around and finally sprang to his feet. Maybe he hoped to inspire us or just did it because that's what John Wayne *would* do, I don't know, but the AKs immediately opened up, he dropped to the prone and we fired back. I was busy shooting, but I think Kell low-crawled up towards the point and saw that they were forming the horseshoe cross fire. When we stopped this volley, he yelled for us to fall back down.

This sounded more logical. We all got up and ran. The machine gun opened up. I saw the muzzle flash as I threw myself down. My God.

The AKs opened up again in back of us and Kell was yelling inaudibly under the noise. He hit someone to pass the signal, we scrambled low-crawling to form a tight circular perimeter. The firing went uninterrupted for over a minute, Fi Bait shouting into his handset.

The machine gunner had fired too soon. If he had waited until we were all running down the hill he may have gotten us all, but he apparently opened up as soon as he saw the bush move. I had just jettisoned the radio and was barely on all fours when it started. He kept spraying back and forth, bullets whizzing and spraying dirt all around, just like in Hollywood, but no one was hit. The final toll was only four Mikes and two Americans.

After we checked fire they did too, just like always. You could still hear them shouting commands. I felt the throbbing nausea. I had seen the muzzle flash, blazing right at me.

Kell crawled over to Silton. Fi Bait screamed for artillery but they couldn't give any. If he hadn't been so excited himself he would have known it; the dinks were too close. I lay there facing the machine gun, looking around. Waiting for something else to happen, approaching the panic.

Fortunately, Kell yelled to open up and I was preoccupied again. As we fired Kell and Sam ran out of the perimeter to our right flank.

There was another minute-long exchange. I shot right at the muzzle flash, as did Fi Bait, who had given up on the radio, and Phil. But the machine gun was beside a teak wood and had a large rock rolled in front of it, there was no way to hit it. I still don't know how he missed so many of us. There was plenty of bush to hide us from sight, but even randomly spraying he should have gotten more.

Kell and Sam had run out to try to circle behind and knock it out. Sam finally did it with a white phosphorous grenade. The muzzle flash stopped a second before the yellow glow and the white streamers fanned out, dissipating in the air like Fourth of July fireworks. The two dinks still alive and screaming, stood up shaking heads and arms. Mouths stretched wide. Sam opened up with his .45 and nailed them both.

The AKs had also stopped by then; everyone had seen the flash. Sam yelled for us to come down. I could hear Kell screaming in pain.

We ran down in a mob, zig-zagging through the bush. The AKs immediately opened up behind us.

Fi Bait and I had already thrown ourselves to the prone, facing back up the hill, when Mastion got it. We all knew that he would be the last American down, and had to hold fire until he made it. He got it, as he *had* to get it after that morning's Hollywood fatalism. Fucked up world.

He was running down beside a Mike. He didn't pause or contort, just fell down on his chest. As the Mikes began passing him we all returned fire. Fuck the Mikes.

But it was all over. The dinks knew we weren't going to charge them and that we would be calling for gunships. If the machine gun had been effective or if they had closed the horseshoe sooner they might have gotten us all. The triple canopy as much as anything saved us. They couldn't get specific targets, just the bush. The ambush must have been a rear-guard element, to stop us while everyone else on the hill escaped. Maybe that's why they didn't use rockets and mortars.

When the AKs finally stopped, we heard Kell screaming from the right, and a Mike or a dink groaning above him.

Phil hit me in the rib and nodded to Sam to put out cover as we ran up to get him. I went without even thinking about it, not knowing what I was doing.

Kell had been hit in the hip and shoulder trying to run out of our first perimeter for the machine gun. When we got there his flat jaw was quivering. Phil gave him morphine and got out the albumin. Kell stared glass-eyed, jaw vibrating and contracting. Phil used a scalpel to cut the pant leg off from the waist down and told me to rip the shirt away from Kell's shoulder. The bullet had gone through the front of his shoulder and lodged in the bone, not bleeding anymore, but the bone raised in a peak where it had broken.

Fi Bait yelled up that he had a medevac coming in. Phil had left his rifle with the others; I had to leave mine beside Kell's pack to help carry him down. We set him by a tree; he passed out but Phil said he would live. He had put a standard dressing on the shoulder, a tourniquet below the hip. He held Kell's head in his arm and wiped the sweat with his left hand.

Two other grunts, brothers from the singing group, went back up with us to carry the Mikes and Mastion down. Four of the nine Mikes had been killed. None of their wounded survived. Phil and I carried Mastion down. Four bullets in his back. When the dinks saw us retreat they must have stood up and nailed him and the Mikes—like shooting deer.

I was numbed and disgusted, like everyone; like always. Fucked up world. But thank God it wasn't me.

This had been the worst and goriest yet. Kell's screaming and shaking his head in delirium when we reached him, four neat holes in Mastion's back. One Mike had gotten it in the back of the skull, through his beret.

Yet I remember the shock this time being less than when Lieutenant Chivington and Fleming had gotten it. I guess a social scientist would call it a progressive adaptation trend in shock intensity. Fuck a bunch of social scientists.

I guess Fi Bait was technically in charge, since he handled the radio. No one cared. We put the bodies in the center of the perimeter and lay prone, ready to fire as we waited for the gunships and medevacs.

Phil didn't bother to take the Mikes' boots off, though he did Mastion's. Just like Lieutenant Chivington and Fleming. KIA tag around the left big toe.

When the two medevacs came in we popped yellow smoke and the gunship escort team kept circling. We put Kell in the first bird and it took off for the field hospital at Pleiku. We later learned that he lived and went to Japan for recuperation, then back to the world. I even got a letter from him at LZ Victory.

The second dust-off stayed hovering almost five minutes, lowering the jungle penetrator for each of the Mike bodies and their gear. After that the Cobras buzzed us and began strafing the peak with mini-guns and rockets. They only made two passes and then circled above us again. Higher called and said we would be immediately extracted, that the gunships were to stay until we were out.

Only three slicks came. Each dropped rope ladders from the sides and we climbed through the triple canopy like LRRPs being extracted. As one bird filled it would join the circling Cobras and another would move in. Fi Bait, Phil, and I were in the last one.

We never found out why they had sent us on that patrol. We never worked with Mikes again, and neither Colonel Fetterman nor Captain Ferris made a speech about Mastion. They didn't even tell us whether there had been something at the top of the hill or whether they thought it had been a freak ambush.

We did have the funeral service though. Mastion had been a Catholic. I had never seen any Catholic religious services but was still not curious. I went only because it was mandatory.

Thank God all patrols aren't like that. I now look back and shake my head. Mastion and Kell—what would have happened if we had backed Mastion up? Poor fucked up bastard.

Yet with any image of Mastion I now also picture the smirk on his face that day he fucked the Yard girl at Plei Jan. I didn't really mourn for him. Unlike for Lieutenant Chivington and Fleming, I felt no compulsion to. I never mourned again, not even for the Anachronism.

That patrol was the last contact made by the first platoon during Bravo company's stay on LZ Jude. The first platoon stayed on the fire base after that, no one left to take it out. Three months of the easy life, sitting at the table each day, the warm glow of the candle in our dry bunker at night, A & C grenadiers, and the brothers singing "Hey Jude." The FO party too never left the fire base.

No other patrol ever went more than five clicks out, and there were only light skirmishes, two or three dinks spotted and killed in the open with all the others—if there were any—always disappearing into the jungle. We kept reporting large vacated bunker complexes and other signs of dinks, but could never find them.

CHAPTER TEN

When word spread that there would be a stand down we talked the entire morning about getting drunk. I blushed when I admitted that I had never been drunk, and everybody laughed and promised that I would be bombed on my ass.

"He'll be better than the Anachronism the first time."

"Nobody could be better than the Anachronism, Big Sam. Henry boy, ever preach a sermon while leanin against the shitter and pukin, in the rain?"

We left the bunkers and wire intact, ARVNs would be moving in.

First Sergeant Ballard had us make five on-line police calls and had his ranking NCOs inspect all bunkers before we packed. Fi Bait wrapped the French bitch in plastic from a battery bag and put her flat against the radio in my pack, stuffing the folded ponchos against it to keep her from getting bent or curled.

Fi Bait used Sam's knife to carve "Fuck you" on the table top.

Captain Ferris had given a briefing the day before and said that we had to get out today: they expected the hill to be smacked in for four days. The fog was indeed already sliding in from Cambodia, yet with sun warm, sparkling the mist as it moved up the valley.

Mortars went first. Captain Ferris kept the first platoon and FO party for the last bird, along with himself and the headquarters personnel. SFC Skinner put his hand on each man's shoulder and counted aloud before letting them file down to the pad—five meters apart, naturally.

After the other two rifle platoons were gone First Sergeant Ballard cupped his hands to scream.

"Okay, let's move out."

He waved his arm, and we filed down past the fifty-caliber bunker for the last time. He and the captain stayed to make one last check of the bunkers. When they came down I guess LZ Jude was officially abandoned by America.

Stand down. As we waited at the pad everyone talked and laughed, all the patrols now vague and irrelevant memories—if still memories at all. It was like the first grade when the teacher takes you down to the auditorium for the assembly before Christmas vacation.

"Gonna get a hot shower, motherfucker."

"Gonna get a piece ass, motherfucker . . ."

"Henry, you're gonna be fucked *up* tonight," said Fi Bait.

I was nervous thinking about getting so drunk I would puke.

"You got a teetotaler there, Phi Beta Kappa?" asked Captain Ferris.

We sat in a semicircle, Captain Ferris and First Sergeant Ballard standing behind at the barbed wire gate. With that voice everyone stopped and looked back. The captain stood resting his forearms on the ammo pouches of his pistol belt, steel pot low on his skull with its blacked-in captain's railroad tracks.

"This time I've got an ordained Baptist preacher, sir. He's worse than the last one, talks about killin a dink for Jesus."

Everyone moaned.

"Sounds like Colonel Fetterman."

Everyone laughed.

"Sir, I don't believe you're cuttin down a superior," said Phil.

"Satank, what am I gonna do with you? It's too bad you're a medic; if you were a grunt, I'd make you my personal body guard, you're so dedicated to upholding the stature of officers."

"Sir, last week Satank told me he wanted to re-up and apply for OCS," said the first sergeant.

Everyone laughed, even Phil.

Just before the shit-hook came it started to drizzle, that fine, indiscernible mist, so thin you couldn't see the splashes in a puddle. Everyone kept joking, but I started to worry, what if the bird couldn't get in for the weather and we had to stay there.

A shit-hook has two sets of synchronized rotors, front and rear, and seats over thirty men. Jacobs served as pad man, waving it down with the football ref motions. When all four wheels had touched, the pitch of the rotors dropped, the whine of the turbines shifting hollow. Everyone was up and running before the gate was all the way down.

I lay behind my ruck watching, squinting into the backwash, waiting for the gate to stop before slipping into the pack. I shot out running, last man, lunging up like a linebacker, with rifle in one hand and holding the steel pot against my head with the other. We all went in running, boots clanking on the steel floor. Everyone held his sixteen pointed down to insure that if a round discharged accidentally it wouldn't hurt the turbines and rotors.

We hovered and pivoted four feet off the ground, I looked out the open gate and got my last glimpse of LZ Jude. I looked for our table but couldn't pick it out, just the blemished Hollywood yellow scuff among endless trees and jungle, and that quickly faded in the cross-currents of white fog.

"Hey Jude." I look back with nostalgia—sitting there at our canopied table, with Cambodia, the hazed blue peaks of Cambodia, in the background, brothers doing requests in the pastel sunset.

It took less than twenty minutes to reach Clarissa. I spent the ride marveling at the cables and pipes overhead, reading the stenciled black paint directions and warnings under each. The turbines made a shrill whistle and were too much to try to talk over. Whenever your eyes met someone else's you would smile.

Approaching Clarissa you could see the terrain come into view above the gate. The crew chief lowered it before we set down, everyone immediately fidgeting to the edge of the seats. When he finally signalled, we charged out like Regulars running out of the landing boats at Utah Beach, with rifles at port arms.

Two deuce-and-a-halfs were parked directly behind, Fi Bait and I ran straight to the second one. I climbed up the wheel but he had to pull me over the stakes because of the weight of radio and pack.

The crew chief leaned out, in his plastic helmet, and flashed the peace sign. A couple guys on our truck whooped like Indians, returning it. I stood against the railing and had to grab Fi Bait for balance as we jerked through the gears, yellow dust floating behind. It was a bright, sunny day at Clarissa, the ground looked like it hadn't rained in weeks.

Bravo company was the last element in the battalion to be extracted. The streets, formed between rows of tents, were already bustling like a frontier mining town. All those grunts, laughing and drinking, some sitting in the dirt, some singing with arms around each other. Fi Bait poked my side and pointed.

"Hey, you motherfucker!"

The Anachronism was standing there leaning on a tent rope, with a coke can. I could feel Fi Bait's face light up, like a little boy who sees his father's car roll up the driveway after work.

The Anachronism immediately turned. "Hey, motherfucker."

"I know that's more than coke in that can, motherfucker." Fi Bait said, twisting his head as we rolled past in the truck.

"Jim Beam. And I got *ice*, motherfucker," the Anachronism said. He walked to the middle of the yellow road, stretched the can up, and gulped.

Fi Bait jumped before we had come to a full stop. I threw

my pack down before jumping—I didn't care if the radio broke or not—and held the rifle out like Geronimo.

The Anachronism extended his hand, "Henry boy."

We shook hands.

Fi Bait took two or three swallows and gave me the can. It did burn going down the throat, but at the same time really tasted sweet. You really did feel your eyes glisten after swallowing, your chest warm.

"Awful free with my liquor ain't you, Phi Beta Kappa? You can go hassle with Bravo company and get your own."

"Kiss my ass." He took the can from me and finished it.

"Motherfucker."

"Kiss my ass. Say, where's your shit?"

"First tent. Bravo's on down."

"Fuck it."

"I hear you guys been havin bad shit, Fi Bait." We stood there in the middle of the road, Fi Bait kicked the can into a tent.

"You wouldn't believe it, John. Un-fucking-real."

"I ain't had no contact since I left you guys."

"Adjust any fire?"

"Just delta-tangos."

As they talked I looked around at the bodies and noise, a few singin groups distinguishable, even a political debate. Just like Saturday in Dodge City, screaming, yelling. One guy tripped over a tent rope and lost his steel pot.

"We better get our shit squared away and see what the lifers are gonna make us do before we can go, John. Where will you be?"

"Fuck, I'll go down with you."

I leaned forward against the pack as we walked, letting my sixteen dangle from the rear sight suitcase handle.

"Oh, I saw Captain Granger, he wants to see all three of us before we move out."

"So fuck him. When we movin out?"

"Shit, you know as much as me. One rumor is tomorrow morning, another, three days."

"If they expect to get me on a bird in the morning they can hang it up. Unless it's a medevac."

"Roger that," said the Anachronism.

We went into the headquarters tent. First Sergeant Ballard and old SFC Skinner were sitting at the folding table drinking Wild Turkey from glasses.

Seeing the first sergeant, we instinctively removed the steel pots and left our packs at the door—though you naturally never let the rifle out of your hand, that's a big Hollywood tradition: "My rifle is my best friend, I eat with him, sleep with him . . ."

"Where do you want your FO party to go, first sergeant?" asked Fi Bait.

They were both smoking cigars, thick green ones. The first sergeant was bald but in excellent physical condition, must have weighed two hundred pounds and would have been a great cadence-caller back at Fort Polk; harsh, raspy voice and that practiced, hard-core-mean look.

"Where'd I want you to go?" He puffed the cigar, "I want you to get a goddamned haircut."

Haircut. So this is stand down. A chance to play stateside soldier. Ballard bobbed his shining head to see the Anachronism, who stood back at the entrance flap.

"What are you doin here, Shoates?"

"I'm with them, first sergeant."

"You go get a haircut too. We got a gook behind the S-4 tent. Only cost you fifty cents a head."

"Then what, first sergeant?" asked Fi Bait. He said it meekly, but how else were you going to talk to a first sergeant, unless you're crazy like Mastion.

"Whadda ya mean, then what?"

"Where should we put our shit?"

"Put it with the first platoon. I'm in charge of the first platoon myself until we get somebody to take it. You guys better check with Echo company too, before you're too drunk to."

"Yes, first sergeant," said Fi Bait. Meekly.

We put the pots on, jerked up the rucks and strode silently into the frontier street.

"I *might* get a haircut, first sergeant," out of ear-shot, "but I fucking *doubt* it."

"Kiss my ass, army!" yelled the Anachronism. "We're hangin it on tonight, troops."

"Better believe it," I said.

The sides of all the tents were rolled up, the posts and crossing lines made it look like a circus just moved into town.

"Here's two more," said Jacobs as we entered.

The sun glowed through the left side, pastel rays like in a movie. It was nearly eleven o'clock.

"Two attach-*ees*," said Fi Bait. "Exempt from whatever it is you got, unless it's good and I know it ain't."

"We gotta keep one man in the tent with the weapons and shit at all times, Fi Bait," said Phil, coke can in hand. "Only hour shifts, though. Hey, Anachronism. How's Alpha company?" throwing up his hand and smiling.

"Sucks ass, doctor."

"No sweat, we'll pull," said Fi Bait. "Where's the liquid?"

Phil pointed to the freezer, Fi Bait and I dropped the packs beside his pallet.

There was nothing in the freezer but coke. You had to get the liquor through an E-6 or higher—E-5s and below can't buy it at the PX—or else pay triple from a bartender at a service club. I gulped and the cold coke seared my throat, more than the Anachronism's Jim Beam had. Standing by the freezer I heard Sam and Phil telling the Anachronism about our two big escapades. You could have sensed that that was it without even hearing, all three looking down and shaking heads.

"Fucking Kell. Lifer Tom," said the Anachronism. "He was fucked up, but he knew the fucking bush."

"I don't know," said Phil. "Damned sure walked into that one. Fuck, what can you say? What the fuck can you say?"

"He was human," said Sam. "So was Mastion."

"Where's the goddamned chow, and who's buying the motherfucking booze?" yelled Fi Bait.

They all turned to us, the conversation turned to getting drunk. Four E-6s from Charlie company were taking the order for liquor and would go to the PX in a jeep after lunch. Fi Bait and I ordered a quart of Jim Beam each. This was put on a platoon order, which Phil delivered to the first sergeant, who in turn submitted a company order to the E-6s.

Someone outside yelled that the deuce-and-a-half making a PX run was ready, and everyone scrambled for the steel pots: "Gettin me some motherfuckin Three Musketeers," "Fucking snack bar, milk shake," as they ran into the frontier street.

Fi Bait and I undid our bed rolls from the aluminum ruck frames and lay on the flat air mattresses until chow. The Anachronism lay on Phil's, which was already blown up. Shadows of the poles and lines streaked the dirt floor, there was one large hole in the roof and dust swirled in the thick ray.

Jacobs was on guard and sat on the ice chest reading somebody's *Playboy*. He let me see it when he finished. I had a good hard-on before even getting to the playmate, which was naturally always the first thing you turned to.

After lunch we picked up clean clothes and four deuce-and-a-halfs conducted shuttles to the showers, one truckload at a time from each company. The showers were freezing and there were four bodies under each spigot but it was still great. I lathered and rinsed several times, new dirt coming off each time. I thought Fi Bait had a good sun tan but he washed it all off. Everyone screamed at how great it was, like kids.

Phil was on guard when we got back, alone in the sunny tent with the passed-down *Playboy.* A messenger from Echo company had been around and said to send the three of us over to Captain Granger ASAP—as soon as possible—if he saw us. Sam was getting our liquor, which had arrived. Phil said he would stay there and watch it until we got back.

I had somehow remembered Captain Granger from the first time in the Old Regulars' Inn as lanky and tall, with that quiet self-confidence, like a textbook New Frontiersman, but as he sat there in the folding chair he struck me as more like Teddy Roosevelt, thick neck and a tow-head. He was reading, sun gleaming off the left stem of his wire-framed glasses. He was reading *Street Without Joy*. CIB.

As I looked at his it suddenly struck me that I too was now CIB-qualified.

He put the book down after we entered. We carried the steel pots under our right arms and lined ourselves before the table, instinctively standing at a modified parade rest, almost like at Fort Polk.

"How's it been, Fi Bait?"

"Shit and piss." Just like talking to an equal. Not even the "sir." "You heard, didn't you?"

"I heard," the captain replied, nodding. "No other platoon's had that heavy a contact and casualties in over a month."

"That must be why John Wayne came out. You hear about that, too?"

"No. Colonel Fetterman?"

"Came out with the fucking chaplain after Lieutenant Chivington got it."

"Booster the old morale?"

Fi Bait nodded. The captain shook his head. "Tell me it's not a great life. Proud to Serve."

He certainly didn't talk like TR, but not the New Frontiersman either. Indeed, looking back he was almost directly parallel to a conscript. Ex-Green Beret. I don't know.

"You guys want a coke? Get one from the chest."

I went back for all three of us. The ice chest was a plastic-lined wooden box, painted infantry blue.

"You want one, sir?" I yelled back.

"No, thanks, Winsted."

The coke again chafed my throat but I gulped away.

"How's Welch, sir?" asked Fi Bait.

"He's okay. Got less than forty days to go."

"Wow, how would you act?" asked the Anachronism.

"Horny," said Fi Bait.

"Which reminds me, Phi Beta Kappa, you want an R&R to Bangkok?"

"Hell yes. But I haven't put in a date yet."

"A guy in recon just cancelled his for lack of funds."

"I've got a grand in Soldiers' Savings at Enari," he said, smiling. "When do I leave?"

"You'll be here for the stand down. Good timing."

Fi Bait howled like a dog. "I ain't left *yet?"* The Anachronism and I both grinned at him. Phi Beta Kappa, a six-year-old kid making his first trip to the zoo.

"Sound perverted, troop. Winsted, has this guy tried to fuck you?"

"I have to fight him off every night, sir. Separate hootches in the boondocks."

"Say, he's a great lay. Thanks for sending him. Beats Shoates all to hell."

"You a dead lay, Shoates?"

"I'm just not promiscuous. That guy'd fuck a Yard if he could."

We were actually talking like in the boonies, not like addressing a captain. It is inconceivable that a captain could talk that way to E-Ms. A lieutenant, if in the boonies, yes; but never a company commander. I don't know. I guess Captain Granger had probably seen his shit the first tour.

"Well, Fi Bait, goin on R&R and gettin your rocks off, think you'll be ready to come into four-deuce when you get back?"

"No, sir."

His tone was suddenly forced, a defensive if not defiant stand.

"No sir, shit," the captain replied. "these guys got it dicked. Stay on the TOC fire base, you'll be in FDC and won't even have to get wet. Nothin to do but write letters and read *Playboy."*

FDC stands for fire direction center, the three or four guys who handle radio communication with the FO and work up data for the guns.

"I'd rather be in the boonies."

"You out of your skull, or drunk already?"

"You know what I mean, sir."

Emphasizing the *sir*. He said it with a straight face. A total reversal from the howling first-grader when he heard about R&R, almost like the movie star standing up for a principle.

I was appalled that he could refuse such an opportunity. A chance to get out of the boondocks for good.

But with time I came to feel the same way. The fighters. You would rather be there with your brothers than even in base camp with clean clothes every week and the whores in Pleiku every weekend. Maybe it's Hollywood, a feeling that you really are a romantic figure, with the pistol belt and rifle, especially after having killed and seen brothers killed. I don't know. At the same time you hated every minute and hated the whole world for having *made* you a fighter . . .

"You once told me your theory was to put college men in the boonies because they would be your best FOs."

"That's right, but you've been out long enough. Winsted can take over."

"You got any college men in four-deuce?"

"You're the only three in the company."

"Swell. Too bad you can't get a couple more Phi Beta Kappas and give these guys RTOs."

Open bitterness.

"Look Fi Bait, after this stand down I'll have a second lieutenant straight from the world running my mortars. I'll need somebody who knows what a fire mission's all about."

"Hard times all over," said Fi Bait.

That was it for spontaneous conversation. The captain pounded the table and pointed at him.

"Look, Phi Beta Kappa . . ."

Fi Bait should have known he was pushing too far. Yet he kept right on, actually interrupting the captain.

"Why don't you bring Shoates in?"

"Because I'm bringin *you* in. How's that grab ya? By the balls?"

Fi Bait rocked on his heels.

"Yes, sir," clearing his throat.

"You've been out longer than any man I've got. After your R&R you'll be fire direction chief in training, and Winsted'll be the Bravo company FO." He was talking as if in a briefing, only his face was red. "I already talked to Captain Ferris. That shake and bake that got it spoke highly of you, Winsted."

I had no chance to reply.

"By the way, did you hear the guy's in Japan and gonna be okay?"

"Good for him," said Fi Bait. "Sir, I don't know how to run an FDC."

"You'll learn."

"If Henry's gonna be an FO you gotta at least make him Spec Four."

"I gotta?"

You might have expected an Article Fifteen or at least twenty-five push-ups right there. Yet Captain Granger just looked at him.

"He's already on the list for next month."

Captain Granger was the exception. He didn't want to put Fi Bait in line, wanted in fact to avoid the situation. I had never heard anyone talk straight to a captain like that. Captains as a group are the worst of all officers. They're ambitious and get their rocks off playing the game. Lieutenants don't care, and majors and above have already made it so they don't have to prove anything to an enlisted man.

He glanced at me and changed the subject.

"You been teachin Fi Bait any history, Winsted?"

"We're collaborating on writing a history of the first of the twenty-second, sir."

"Drive on."

"You gonna let me stay in Bravo company for the stand down, sir?"

"Yes, Fi Bait, but Echo company's having a barbecue at 18:00 hours, you'll all three be there. So will my other two FOs. You'll leave for base camp day after tomorrow."

"When did we get two others?" asked the Anachronism.

"Both shake and bake eleven charlies."

"Sir, I bet Henry knows more about FOin than both of them put together. Why don't they make him an instant buck sergeant?"

"Fi Bait, don't hassle me!" pounding the table, "You know I see all that horse shit, just like you. You *know* I do. I'm in the fucking army just like you. Gimme a drink of fucking coke."

He gulped several times and dropped the can on the yellow dirt.

"I emptied it, how's that grab ya?"

Pointing his finger again, "Lucky for you, Mr. Phi Beta Kappa, that I'm Mister *Nice* Guy."

"Okay, nice guy."

We left as if on cue.

I don't know how to figure Captain Granger. He was disillusioned, but you know there was still that dreamy Hollywood image of the young man doing something noble with his life: "Duty, Honor, Country," John Kennedy, Cold Warrior—he still *wanted* to hold the image.

By now the liquor was flowing and the boys were whooping it up out in the streets of Dodge City. We passed Big Sam and a brother from Delta company arguing between Cassius Clay and Joe Louis. Someone had puked at the corner of one tent and one of the dogs—a lot of units in the rear have mascot dogs——sniffed it and had a coke can thrown at him. He yelped and ran into the tent only to be screamed at and further harassed.

"Motherfuck," said Fi Bait, kicking the dust as we walked. "Four-deuce. That's almost like bein a base camp commando."

"I can't *believe* I hear a complaint," said the Anachronism. "Goin on R&R and gettin out of the boondocks at one fell swoop and you're *complainin?* Sorry fucker. Christ, in three days you'll be in Bangkok fuckin, and me and Henry'll be jackin off leeches."

Fi Bait laughed and slapped the Anachronism's shoulder. "Don't torture yourself. Say, I'll whisper your name in her ear one time. An-ach-ron-ism."

"She'll think it's a big word for blow job," I said, and we all laughed.

It must have been two or three o'clock by then, the sun gleaming aluminum in that cloudless pale sky, Dodge City dust almost stagnant in the heat and several grunts with shirts open and sweating, dog tags rattling on chests.

The tent was cooler, and nearly the whole first platoon was inside. There were three card games. Phil and Jacobs sat on the ice chest arguing over the names of Hopalong Cassidy and the Lone Ranger's horses.

"Medic!" yelled Fi Bait. "In three days I'll be in Bangkok."

"Yeah, and I'll be ridin the Lone Ranger's horse down to Saigon."

"R&R, motherfucker. Ask these guys."

"Fucker's goin on R&R," said the Anachronism. "Not only that, he's goin into four-deuce."

"You leavin Bravo company?" asked Sam. He was in one of the card games and smoking a Hava Tampa, and turned to look at Fi Bait.

Fi Bait nodded.

"Gonna be a shammin motherfucker," said Phil.

"Shammin, shit, Where's our liquor? Bunch of glorified commandos."

"They're in my ruck there."

The Anachronism pulled the bottles out, we sat in a circle with legs folded like Indians.

"Heave us some cokes, Doctor," yelled Fi Bait. Phil threw the cans down the tent, over everyone's head—everyone was either sitting or lying. We took out our canteen cups, the Anachronism utilized Phil's, and we began with Fi Bait's bottle.

"Here's to four-deuce, gentlemen. May it appreciate the true fortune of having a Phi Beta Kappa directing its fire."

I could barely tell there was liquor in mine, the coke in Captain Granger's tent must have left a coating in my mouth.

"May it appreciate its two unsung B.A. Baptists of the boondocks," clanking the tin cups together.

"To the Anachronism, the poet, the last grand and concerned human," I said.

"You guys having a circle jerk?" yelled Sam.

"That's a *roger,*" said Fi Bait. "One last time."

"You're gonna be a shammin motherfucker, Fi Bait."

"Shammin nothin. Glorified commandos. Goddamned pussies."

"You insane, FO? You're gettin out of the boondocks."

"But it ain't the right way to leave, Big Sam," drinking, "I won't get to pop smoke."

It is traditional for every grunt leaving the bush for the last time—for the freedom bird, home—to get the glory ride. The slick buzzes the fire base with everyone below waving and then arches up like Steve Canyon, popping two smoke grenades and dropping them to the jungle as you leave. Laughing at the world, and leaving for good.

"You ain't in Hollywood," I said. "You should be thankful."

"Okay, Hollywood. Hey *Jacobs,"* he yelled, "Topper and motherfucking Silver, respectively."

"That's right!" yelled Phil.

"Buttercup, motherfucker," said Jacobs.

"Fuck you."

"Fuck you, medic."

We finished Fi Bait's bottle and a third of mine before supper, mixing it heavy with coke. I kept asking if I was drunk—how do you know when you're really drunk?—sitting up straight on the ground, legs crossed like an Indian.

"Sure, my head's thick and light, but I still know what I'm doin."

"You're *supposed* to, even if you're drunk. You ain't drunk though. Tonight you'll low-crawl to that fuckin air mattress."

Walking to the Echo company barbecue I was staggering. I remember thinking I'm drunk, by God, I really am drunk. But I was surprised at how clearly my mind worked. I had never seen a real drunk except in the movies, and it really was just like in the movies. You could feel yourself weaving and talking thick and loud. After it was over I remembered everything that had happened and was appalled at what a hangover really is, so much worse than any television commercial, with dry heaves, diarrhea.

The Echo company barbecue was being held behind the S-4 tent. Barbecued steaks, with the first cook's own special sauce. We had carefully wrapped my bottle in a poncho liner and given Sam, who was on guard—Bravo and all the other companies were also having mandatory barbecues—instructions to guard it with his life.

"Four-deuce, behold I give unto thee a new computer," cried the Anachronism as we stepped into line, spreading his arms with paper plate in one hand and plastic knife and fork in the other.

"A computer like none ye hath ever beheld," I said, with an arm around Fi Bait.

A gook KP cut through the line with a tray of meat on top of his head. It was an old man, hunchbacked with a white, Ho Chi Minh beard and baggy shorts, yellow, rubber shower thongs.

"What ho, what ho, me lads," cried Fi Bait. He pointed at him, finger waving and circling. "Be it gook or be it dink?"

"Yea verily it be gook," said the Anachronism. "Know ye not that were it dink we would needs be pounce upon him, and smite him, verily?"

"But yea verily, ye must spare the gook, even as I hath bade you smite the dink."

"Yea verily," I said.

Echo company was sober, or at least not as drunk as us. They all eyeballed us, standing in line muttering to each other.

"Yea though I walk through the valley of the shadow of death," said Fi Bait.

"I shall fear no mortar," I said.

"For they art piss-poor shots," yelled someone from Echo company.

The whole company laughed, we were taken aback and made no reply. Smart-assed bastards.

"Well done my friend," the Anachronism yelled up to the cook.

"Well done, my noncombatant friend," said Fi Bait.

"That one," I said, pointing to the biggest one. They had twenty or thirty steaks cooking at once. There were also french fried potatoes and orange jello with fruit in it—help yourself with the tin ladle—also a ten-gallon mess hall pot with grape koolaid.

Most of the company was already eating; some going

back for seconds as we got out of line. There was a dirt yard between S-4 and the next sector of tents. We sat on the side by ourselves, Indian style.

I had never pictured Captain Granger getting drunk. He had that image of total self-respect, self-pride. Yet you might say it was concern for self-respect, for *wanting* to preserve it, in the face of everything, that made him drink.

The Anachronism spotted him staggering from the shitter, poked Fi Bait with his elbow, and pointed.

"Hey, Captain Granger! Come here, you motherfucker," yelled Fi Bait.

No one talked to a company commander like that, even if he was drunk.

Captain Granger stopped and whirled, like the gunfighter spinning to slap leather.

"Is that a fucking Phi Beta Kappa I hear?" yelling down the street.

"Over here," waving.

"A Phi Beta Kappa and his two fucking college cohorts. Fuck you!"

He reeled and pushed his arms through the air for steering. Echo company was quiet and eyeballed him. He finally dropped before us, right leg flying up and groaning as the side of his back hit the dirt, rolling back into a sitting position, slapping Fi Bait's shoulder with one hand and mine with the other.

"Lemme tell ya, troops, I'm fucked up. And I don't *give* a motherfuck."

"You're all right, sir. You'd be all right if you weren't in the army." Fi Bait set his plate down and leaned to shake his hand. "You're okay, sir."

"That's right, sir," said the Anachronism.

I mumbled and nodded, mouth full of food.

"Gee thanks, men. Thanks a lot."

His head dangled and swung between Fi Bait's plate and mine.

"You guys know I'm not a lifer. I'm not a motherfuckin lifer. I'm fucking OCS. It's the motherfucking world, Fi Bait," slapping both of us and taking a deep breath. "You better forget you ever saw me this way. Look at my troops over there."

"See my little troopies? They're gonna get a bad image of me, gonna lose respect for me. Well *fuck* 'em. You know what I mean? Why the fuck should I care?"

"I know, sir. Lemme tell ya, you're fucking disillusioned. That's what it is."

The Anachronism and I nodded vigorously.

"Shh," putting his fingers on his lips.

"Don't let nobody hear me let you talk that way. I get a reprimand, you probably get an Article Fifteen from me. Fi Bait, I'm an okay guy, you know I am."

"You're squared away, sir. I'll *shoot* any fucker says you ain't. You're the only officer I ever saw I ever respected. And I ain't kiddin. I mean it."

"That goes for me, too."

"Me too, sir," I said.

"Thanks guys. Thanks a lot." I wasn't sure whether he was crying or not. "You guys are okay. Winsted, you're gonna be a good man. I knew you would be. FO's the most important job."

He hit Fi Bait's shoulder. "But I hadda bring y'in, Fi Bait. I hadda."

"I know, sir."

"Thanks, Fi Bait. Thanks," slapping his shoulder again. "I gotta get outa here 'fore some fuckin officer comes and sees me fraternizin with you guys."

"We understand, sir," said Fi Bait.

He walked back towards the shitter, with the sun setting ahead of him. When he had gone, Echo company quickly came to life again.

"There goes one fucked up guy, Fi Bait," said the Anachronism. "I never, never saw an officer like him."

"He's more fucked up than fucking Kell," said Fi Bait.

We left our garbage lying in the dirt and moved out for the first platoon's tent and our liquor. I hadn't eaten half of my steak. All three of us had the steel pots' sweat bands pushed back above our foreheads, walking—staggering—abreast along the tents.

Everyone from Bravo company was out at their barbecue, even Sam, the guard.

"Wanna go to the Bravo barbecue?" asked Fi Bait.

"No, let's stay here," said the Anachronism.

"Nice quiet atmosphere. Only chance you'll ever have to escape."

Fi Bait got my bottle and the canteen cups out, I brought three cokes from the ice chest. We again sat in the circle, legs crossed like Indians.

"To Bangkok," said Fi Bait.

"To cunnelinkus, or whatever the fuck it is," said the Anachronism.

"Fucking pervert."

"How much money ya takin, Fi Bait?" I asked.

"Fucking grand. Get my fucking mother some bronzewear and shit. Probably get a big teakwood elephant."

"Get yourself some threads," I said.

"Hell yes."

"Be sure you bring a picture, motherfucker," said the Anachronism. "Bet you get a pig."

"Bet I do better'n the French bitch."

"Sorry fucker. Hey Fi Bait, y'oughta see this fuckin red leg FO in Alpha company—second lieutenant and can't hump the fuckin boonies. Even with no radio or sixty rounds."

"Fucking red leg. Might as well be noncombatant. I bet he stays on the fire base and makes you go on every patrol, don't he?"

"Course he does. They say he's only been on one patrol, and been with the company four months."

"How's Alpha company?"

"Ain't like the old first platoon."

"Can't beat old Bravo. Right Henry? Here's to *Bravo* company." He yelled it, and chug-a-lugged.

"Here's to the Regulars."

It was dark when we finished my bottle, and we were leaning and patting each other as we talked, telling each other how it was and asking if the other understood.

"Okay, men, here's what we do. Each take three cokes and put 'em in our pockets. Then we get the fucking

Anachronism's bottle and take off by ourselves. Fuck these Regulars and their barbecues."

"Good copy," said the Anachronism. "Nobody knows how it is but us. We gotta stick together. Right, Henry?"

"Right. We're the only three."

Jungle fatigues have big two-button pockets low on the sides of the legs. The coke was cold against my legs as I walked.

Troops were now lying on the dirt at the end of the tent area, waiting for the movie. The screen was made of a bed sheet stretched on a wooden frame built for the occasion. Big Sam was standing in back of the crowd, standing alone with his audience of six or seven brothers lying in a circle around him. He sang "Lonesome Valley." Just like Leadbelly, wailing: "You gat to wa-alk, that lonesome valley." The only time I ever heard Big Sam use the Hollywood Black dialect. "You gat to wa-alk it by yourself . . ."

"We don't need their fuckin movie," said the Anachronism.

"Fuck no," I said.

The Anachronism's tent was empty and we used a P-38 to take the tops off the first coke cans. I had always thought a P-38 was a World War II airplane, but in the Action Army it's a C-ration can-opener. Each can sprayed with the first puncture, from being shaken as we walked. We drank enough coke to leave space in the cans for liquor, and the Anachronism poured. He screwed the cap back on the bottle and put it in his big leg pocket before we moved out.

All the tents now had the sides rolled down. Some had lanterns burning inside, casting a white beam before us and the flame roaring as we passed. We were soon out of the battalion area and headed for the heart of Clarissa. After the last two tents we crossed a ditch and ran into a winding blacktop road.

I knew we were all really drunk now, almost yelling to speak, hugging each other, staggering, the whole bit. But it was great. It was great to be able to hug somebody who knew, and to talk like in a movie.

"Motherfuck the whole goddamned world," said Fi Bait,

grabbing my collar and with his free hand, spinning me around to face him.

"Fuckin Phi Beta Kappa, Henry. And here I am. My fuckin father never went to high school."

He paused to drink, gasping to speak. "Fuckin father, Henry, he writes me these letters 'Proud of you, son. You're servin your country, and you'll do things someday that I never had the opportunity to do.' "

"Fuckin mine too!" I cried, slapping his shoulder.

Then the Anachronism.

"Listen, hold it."

He had stepped in front of us. "Hold it. Listen, listen, my fuckin Uncle Malcolm, fuckin Alamo Scout, Baptist preacher, fuckin writes that God loves me and has a wonderful plan for my life. Fuckin *prays* for me."

"God damn it, Henry. You tell me it ain't fucked up. Tell me it ain't," shaking me with one hand and the liquor spilling from the other.

"Nobody knows but us," I said. I was shaking my head in sympathy. Poor Anachronism.

"Mother-*fuck* you, world," yelled Fi Bait.

He threw his can at a tree, missed and nearly fell, then cupped his hands over his mouth.

"Mother-*fuck* you, world," staring up at the sky, his neck taut.

The Anachronism threw his can and repeated the plea; I chug-a-lugged mine and did the same.

"Mother-*fuck* you, world." I was reeling.

"Okay, bartender," said Fi Bait in a low tone.

We huddled in the road and each pulled out another coke. We poured half the coke right onto the asphalt instead of drinking it, and the Anachronism emptied the bottle between the three cans and put it back in his pocket.

"And here's to Lifer Tom Kell," screamed Fi Bait, "*Fuck* you, Kell, you dumb bastard."

He was yelling himself hoarse.

"Here's to Chivington," I said. "Fuck you, lieutenant," immediately turning to Fi Bait and leaning into his face. "Say, you think his ancestor was at Sand Creek, Fi Bait? Nits make lice."

"A good point. But hold it, hold it," staring into his coke can. "I think I got three gulps left, gentlemen. Here's your grand toast. Here we go."

The Anachronism and I raised our cans waiting.

"Here's to the Now Generation. *Fuck* you, Now Generation." Drinking and holding them out again.

"Here's to students," I said. "Fuck you, students."

"And Kennedy. Fuck you, Kennedy! Fuck you, New Frontier."

We all whooped and yelled.

"Ask not . . ."

I remember starting to sing "What a Friend We Have in Jesus."

"*Fuck* you, Jesus!" cried the Anachronism.

"*Fuck* you," screamed Fi Bait.

He took the bottle from the Anachronism's pocket. We were on a curve in the road and a shit-hook was parked on a pad below us. Fi Bait wound up like a baseball pitcher, screaming "mother-*fuck* you" as he threw. It fell short but we all whooped like cowboys hearing the glass break.

"Mother-*fuck* you!" we all screamed.

Fi Bait threw his can, we followed the example. There was still liquid in mine and it got all three of us. We staggered on with arms around each other, singing, screaming the obscenities, a few historical references to TR and Aguinaldo. The Anachronism, of course, brought in the fucking Baptists.

We ended up flagging a jeep, a night driver making CQ checks, and he delivered us to the Regulars' area. I don't know where we would have wound up if we'd kept walking on that road. Everybody else was still at the movie. The Anachronism hugged each of us when he left him at the Alpha company tents.

"My brothers. Only we know."

As soon as I lay down I puked thin, brown liquid. I just lifted my head and puked right where I lay, wiping where my head would go with my right sleeve. I put the poncho liner over it and immediately went to sleep, without even blowing the mattress up.

In the morning I had the dry heaves and GI shits. The

smell of last night's puke made me want to puke again, even as I moaned desperately, trying to ease the quivering stomach. I was one of the first out to the shitter. I stayed there over an hour, moaning and groaning. Fi Bait said he had a hangover, but didn't puke and shit like me. Jacobs was the only other dry heaver from our tent.

That day was spent recovering and drawing needed gear: new boots, canteens, helmet liners. I cleaned the radio and got a spare handset. After lunch both chaplains held services for the whole battalion in the yard where they had had the movie—first the Catholic, then the Protestant.

I gave the French bitch back to Fi Bait and he gave me his compass. We would move out for the pads at seven-thirty next morning, CA to an ARVN camp called LZ Victory.

CHAPTER ELEVEN

First Sergeant Ballard personally got the troops out, at five-thirty. Even had a formation and on-line police call after breakfast.

We moved to the pad in deuce-and-a-halfs, at least fifteen of them all together. I again stood cramped against the rail, and waved my steel pot.

"Drive on, Phi Beta Kappa."

"Keep a tight asshole, FO," dropping the razor in his steel pot. As he spoke a glob of shaving cream fell from his chin.

"Knock off a piece for me," said Sam.

"Hope you get the clap!" yelled the medic.

Fi Bait grinned big and gave us the finger, still holding it as we turned from the tents onto the blacktop.

You shouldn't call it a CA, just a helicopter ride. LZ Victory was a permanent fire base, already secured by an ARVN battalion, far from a real CA, into the jungle. We didn't even have gunships, didn't need them.

We were to hump out from Victory on a search and destroy. Captain Ferris had given me a map the night before and told me that the first platoon and I would be the headquarters element. First Sergeant Ballard would go back to Enari—he probably personally created some business to tend so he wouldn't have to hump with us. Alpha and Charlie would also search and destroy, Delta would set up at Victory with the TOC, as would four-deuce, recon, and the four 81 platoons—81s rarely ever humped, more hassle than it was worth. You could get artillery support quicker than they could lay the tubes and get a round hanging.

After the ride, Phil and I dropped our rucks at the CP and went to the four-deuce area to look out at the river. It was low and swift, a rapids at a bend past the village. We couldn't see the village for the bush on the other bank, could make out the women stooping in the rapids to wash clothes.

The monsoon was over at LZ Victory; yellow dirt tramped so hard that there was no dust, even when a shit-hook came in. It was really two big rectangular perimeters, linked by two fighting trenches, like a box kite. The ARVN half had a building in the middle with a tin roof and flag pole.

"Bravo company!"

We turned, SFC Skinner was standing by the CP bunker, waving. "Bravo company, form by the CP. Form by the CP."

"That dumb fucker," said Phil as we walked back. He kicked a C-ration fruit can along the bleached ground.

"Better him than Ballard."

"Huh, you ain't said shit."

The CP had a concertina fence to keep dink sappers out, complete with a gate of engineer stakes wired together. The company clustered outside, and Captain Ferris came out lighting a cigar. He told everyone to spread in an arc so they could hear.

"Okay men, just like you knew they would, the army's fucked up again. We ain't movin out until tomorrow. They're gonna put air strikes and night fire around the route of march." He dropped the lighter into his leg pocket. "So that means we'll be here tonight, and so will all the other rifle companies. We'll get hot chow from the artillery mess tent. Move out in the morning for sure. Any questions?"

"How long we gonna be out, sir?" asked a sergeant from the third platoon.

"Twenty days and nineteen nights."

There was a low murmer, but not over five or six voices.

"After that we're comin back here and secure the fire

base and Alpha's gonna hump awhile. You're lucky, Alpha company's gonna be out sixty days before they come in. Terrain here's a lot better than Jude, as you probably noticed from the birds. They really don't expect us to find much, just want a sweep. They haven't had any intelligence from this AO in a long time."

"The mission's large-scale reconnaissance," said SFC Skinner.

Captain Ferris eyeballed him, puffing his cigar at the interruption. It was a thick green cigar, like the ones First Sergeant Ballard and the SFC had had during stand down.

"That's right, Sergeant Skinner," he stammered. "Be nice if we can take some prisoners."

"Okay, it's gonna be a whorehouse tonight with all four rifle companies in. We're gonna set up two-man hootches out there in the pad area, any birds come in they'll set down outside the wire. Won't have no bunker guard tonight, Alpha company's securin."

He flicked ashes. "Okay, don't all go ape shit at once, but the old man says you can go down to the river after chow. One platoon at a time, in hour shifts. There's whores down there . . ."

Immediate roar, like the interruption of a convention speaker on television.

The captain grinned and waved his arms for calm.

"There's whores down there," raising his voice, "but needless to say, enter at your own risk."

A laugh from the grunts.

"If you're gonna knock off a piece do it before you go in swimmin." He looked at his watch. "Right now wait till Charlie and Delta companies get in, then go out and set up your hootches. Get chow at the red leg mess tent. Platoon leaders check with me before you let 'em loose. Silton. Where's Spec-four Silton?"

"Here, sir."

"You're in charge of the first platoon. You guys go down first, but make sure everybody's hootch is up and check it out with Sergeant Skinner before you go down. Each man *will* have steel pot, weapon, and one bandolier as he leaves the wire. Got that?"

"Yes, sir," said Sam.

"Okay. That's it."

He started to leave but turned back to the troops from inside the TOC's wire.

"I got a bet with Alpha company CO that he has more guys come down with the clap than we do."

"You lose, sir," said Phil.

"Satank, I know you're gonna be the first case."

We dispersed, most of us rubbing our hands over the whores. I looked off and saw a shit-hook beating in, the third shift of TOC and mortar personnel.

"You gonna knock off a piece?" I asked Phil.

"*Hell* yes. I ain't had a piece since I left the world."

"You got a rubber?"

Mind heavy but trying to calculate—I don't know exactly what—eyeballing the yellow dirt as we walked.

"Shit, I'm the medic. I dispense 'em to everybody else. You want one?"

He stopped walking and eyeballed.

"Wait till we get down there. See what they look like," staring down.

He must have smiled a full minute. That impish paternal smile. Actually tapped my shoulder with his rifle as we walked on. I was pissed off.

We stopped behind one of the artillery's sleeping bunkers, dropped the packs and sat against the sandbag wall. The sandbags were cold in the shade, tingling on your back. I deliberately closed my eyes, didn't want him pressing about the whores.

"This looks like the spot," said Sam as he and Jacobs approached. "Nice shade."

"Fuckin heat. Gimme the monsoon back," said Jacobs.

"So fuck it," said Phil. "It's a hardship tour."

"Ain't it though," said Sam. "Gonna fuck, medic?"

"*Hell* yes."

I opened my eyes and saw Sam unfolding the sixty's bipod. He set it in the sun. White streak reflecting on the barrel. Jacobs sat next to me.

"Mmm, good old shade, nice cool sandbags."

"Yeah," I said.

"Gonna get laid, FO?" asked Sam.

"Don't know," with my eyes closed.

"Sh. You're like old Jacobs, goddamned cherry boy."

I glanced sidelong at Jacobs, holding an unconcerned face—trying to and hoping I was.

"Shit," said Jacobs. "I ain't messin with them goddamned gooks. Got fifty-seven varieties of disease."

"Just a cherry boy, goddamned bashful cherry boy."

Phil poked my side.

"You go down there and get yourself messed up. Go ahead."

Jacobs now had his eyes closed. The conversation soon ended. I thought of Fi Bait and R&R, mind floating with images of copulation. College girls, I fell asleep. Phil kicked me to wake me for chow.

The first platoon set up hootches in the corner between the concertina of our perimeter and the trench on the river side. There was a two-foot-high sandbag wall in front of the trench, ideal cover if hit from the river, and we could easily jump if need be. The third platoon's lieutenant tried to claim it, but Big Sam told him that Captain Ferris had ordered us to set up here; of course he hadn't.

We had to use engineer stakes for the frame, and I dented my steel pot pounding my post into the hard ground. SFC Skinner came down to check before we were finished.

"Lookin good first platoon," he said. "Tell you what, you take off soon as you're finished; don't bother checkin with me. Just be back by two-thirty, okay?"

We all nodded. He was smiling, obviously feeling good at giving us a special privilege. It wasn't yet twelve-thirty; we would be ready to go in five minutes at most.

"Just want your word, men. You be back at two-thirty."

We nodded again.

He motioned his hands like an umpire signalling safe. "That's all. If you see ARVNs though, don't mess with them. They sell you pot, you get in trouble. You don't need that. Okay?"

He turned and left without an answer.

"Thanks, sergeant," yelled Sam.

He waved and kept going without looking back.

Old SFC Skinner. He had been a grunt in the Korean war. Fucked up old bastard.

We draped the olive-drab towels around our necks and walked single file through the perimeter, bandoliers over the shoulders, Big Sam leading with his .45 holstered. Whores. Would I do it? *Hell* yes. What would it be like, though? Would it be worth it? *Hell*, you're in the land of the Nam. But would it be worth it?

One of the four-deuce tubes was getting ready for a settling round. Three guys standing on the base plate, ears plugged. One guy holding the white illumination round over the barrel.

"Round hangin!"

Everyone stopped and automatically grabbed their ears, I tucked the rifle in my armpit and crouched as the guy dropped the round. He ducked away and covered his own ears as it went. Mighty four-deuce—jolting the guys off the base plate and blue smoke pouring from the barrel.

I turned and looked back at the gun crew as we went on. Just before we reached the wire he yelled again, "Round hangin!" Everyone again grasping ears just as it went.

I heard the squad leader yell "Looks good FDC," as we descended to the path.

My heart beat faster with each step. We walked about a hundred meters, and there they were, standing right before us. They were wading knee-deep in the water but stopped and waved. I could feel my throat tighten, and my eyes bulged; thoughts immediately reversed. They were *pigs*. My God, how could anybody?

There were five of them; they kept waving and smiling as we walked down. They wore mini-skirts and heavy face make-up; but barefooted, and gross. My God. They came out of the water running, giggling. We stopped in the line of march; it was almost like being inspected by a drill sergeant, standing there in the ranks.

Squeezing the cheek, or rubbing the hips against your groin—"me boocoo horny, Joe"—winking and nodding to the bushes.

The ugliest of all stopped in front of me. Four feet tall

and cross-eyed, gross swollen pudgy legs rubbing together at the knees. She felt my balls with one hand and rubbed my cheek with the other. Moaning, winking. I didn't get a hard-on, just stood there in amazement. I should have laughed, but it was too unreal. She must have tried over a minute, lifting the skirt and pressing against me, squeezing my balls and pulling as she moaned. She raised her ass and snorted when she finally moved on, just like the one at the first convoy point at Pleiku. But I *should* have done it with the one back at Pleiku.

None of us spoke as the whores went through the ranks. Everyone else must have been just as numbed as I was. Finally Sam looked back at Phil.

"You got rubbers, medic?"

Phil grinned and pulled two boxes out of his leg pocket.

"You're an animal," Jacobs said to Sam.

"Animal, shit."

Jacobs walked out of line towards the shore, and a few guys followed. The whores yapped for them to come back. "Oh Joe, boocoo horny."

"I'm goin swimmin, brother. Mess with them nasty-assed whores, shit."

I followed Jacobs, relieved, and wanting to laugh out loud. My God.

It turned out that Sam was the only one. Not even old Phil could lower himself. I was ashamed of Sam—though I had no right to judge; if you want to do it, better do it while you can. Jacobs and Phil teased him as he gave her the five dollars and took her hand. It was the cross-eye that had tried for me.

"You *must* be horny," said Phil.

"Shit."

"You're crazy, Sam," said Jacobs. "Fifty-seven varieties of disease."

"You never mind, motherfucker."

He jerked the girl's arm, making her scream as he dragged her to the bushes.

"You ain't gonna?" I asked Phil. I sat down to pull the boots off.

"You got to be kiddin, hillbilly."

We were all in swimming when Sam came back, buttoning his pants.

"Hey, machine gunner. Was it worth it?" yelled Phil.

"Shut up, motherfucker."

He sat down to undress. That was the only time I ever saw Sam like that. Face drawn, eyes glistening, and the lips pressed tightly together, purple.

He was standing to pull his pants off when his whore came back from the bushes. She giggled and muttered in gook, and touched his naked ass with her foot. We all laughed, that is, most of us; I didn't, and I don't think Jacobs did.

Sam whirled and threw a rock at her.

"Bitch!" he screamed.

The rock hit her in the breast, she held it with both hands and started crying like a child. Probably hit the very nipple. The other whores soon huddled around her, muttering at Sam as they walked her up the trail, comforting her. Cross-eyes. She was crying real tears, heaving for breath.

"Goddamned whore," said Sam as he stepped out of his pants.

We had all become silent when he threw the rock, just standing in the waist-deep water and staring. You could feel the tension. Everyone deliberately avoided looking at him.

Finally Phil splashed Jacobs, starting a water fight, and we were again loose. Jacobs couldn't swim and constantly got his head dunked.

After ten or fifteen minutes three new whores came down the trail. We stopped and stared. They waved, wiggling their hips and playing with their tits. Mini-skirts and make up—gook whores.

"Hit the road, gooks," yelled Phil.

"Move on!" yelled Sam, and we all started yelling and motioning. They walked on leisurely, strolling, sneering at us. We went back to splashing, seeing who could stay under longest.

As we walked back I felt great, not only from swimming and playing, but satisfied, and somehow proud. I was glad

I hadn't done it with the whores and laughed at myself for ever having made a big deal out of it. I think one of the first five had cow shit between her toes.

I thought of Mastion and the Yard at Plei Jan. And Sam, I don't know. It was a shock to see him do it. I thought back to that first convey, Kell and Mile-wide. Sam and Cross-eye. And each's own revulsion afterwards. Christ.

"How are they?" asked somebody from four-deuce as we filed back in.

"Paradise," said Phil. "Worth a month's pay."

The guy whooped. "I ain't down there fuckin *yet?"*

That night I didn't get to sleep until well after midnight because of the night fire. Every two minutes, "Round hangin!" and the shot ringing and echoing. It was more hassle to plug your ears than it was worth. At ten the 105s started, they were louder, and no one even gave a "round hangin."

Phil and I cursed to each other and ended up bullshitting on into the night. Phil went out to find a shitter at one point and I lay back, thinking about the day—the whores, the helicopter ride from Clarissa, the door gunner. The door gunner had leaned over and tapped me as we lifted off, grinning and yelling in my ear. "I got twenty-seven days!" He lowered the green visor and closed his sixty's feed tray. Twenty-seven days, how would I act?

In the morning we shaved, ate breakfast with the red legs again and drew a case of Cs per man. We left the frames of the hootches standing and were all ready to move up to the CP when SFC Skinner came down for the inevitable police call. Charlie company was also set up on the pad. We started at our concertina, and they started at the gooks', crossing in the middle.

"Git it *all*, men."

Most of Bravo company threw it over the wire into the ARVN perimeter. Charlie company marched single file to the sump, around the ARVN perimeter.

We again formed by the CP's concertina, only this time saddled up and ready to go. Captain Ferris reemphasized in his briefing tht it should be easy humping and that he wanted to try for some prisoners. Jacobs asked the first question.

"Are we gonna get mail, sir?"

"Letters and the *Stars and Stripes* with the resupply bird every four days. Packages'll be held back here." Looking at his watch. "Lieutenant Jackson, go over to the ARVNs and pick up that Kit Carson Scout."

Lieutenant Jackson was in charge of the third platoon. Kit Carson scouts are former VC or NVA who surrender to use their jungle wile and prowess in their country's proper cause. It turned out though that Lieutenant Jackson had a communications problem and couldn't find a scout or a gook who knew what the word scout meant. We were scheduled to move out at eight o'clock, so he hung it up and came back without him.

"Fuck it," said Captain Ferris.

"Okay, everybody double-check your canteens and take five before we move out."

Everyone dropped the rucks but remained standing, machine gun rounds glistening across the grunts' chests, cross-slung like Poncho Villa. That is the most impressive image of all, except the helicopters.

After the break he gave the signal without speaking, we saddled up and formed into the file of march. The third platoon moved out first, point man with the Remington .12 gauge, then headquarters and the second platoon. The guy walking point for our element had less time in country than me. Probably had Mastion's very shotgun.

SFC Skinner stood by the TOC's concertina and eyeballed as we filed by. We crossed the river at the place where the first platoon had confronted its whores.

On the other shore the three elements split. Each had two radios, one on Command Alpha with the TOC and one on the company internal push. That kind of humping is tricky. In thick bush a smart dink can draw each element's fire and end up having the company fighting no one but itself. That's why the second radios.

Fortunately the bush here wasn't that bad, not like Jude. Low hills with sapling trees, more like forest than jungle, no bamboo, no vines to duck, the point man didn't even need a machete. You could see thirty or forty feet all around, the sun screened pastel through the trees. I could see the third platoon moving on our flank. The technique would be for headquarters to form a perimeter at each check point, the other two elements to recon for a five hundred meter radius and report back.

We had walked an hour when the captain gave the first signal to halt. We stood there in line instead of forming a perimeter. My instinct was that the point man had found something and was checking it out, so I pulled the map from me leg pocket and started checking for targets. Captain Ferris was on the internal radio.

We just stood there in line, most unusual, and soon began mumbling to each other.

Captain Ferris finally passed it up for the point man to come back, gave him the instructions, and immediately made the signal to move out. But we struck out due west of the proper route of march, and I wondered what *was* up, why the detour. I was suddenly conscious that I was the FO, and kept checking the map for targets.

We walked right into the third platoon's perimeter. Captain Ferris spread his arms, like a swimmer's breast stroke, and the two elements mingled to form a bigger perimeter. I was still studying the map as I squatted beside the captain.

"What's up, sir? Want me to work up a grid?"

"No, we're all right, Winsted."

He eyeballed Lieutenant Jackson, who approached with the grunt, holding the guy by the shirt collar. I had the feeling I was the only person who didn't know what was going on, like when you've been daydreaming and listen to the conversation around you for the first time.

Then I noticed the brother, against a teakwood with Phil and the third platoon medic working on him.

"I didn't see it, sir," said the grunt, pleading to the captain, who was sitting like an Indian; the rest of us, Captain Ferris, his RTO, Lieutenant Jackson and his RTO, and me, kneeling and staring.

"How could you have missed it, when the guy right in

front of you went down?" The captain spoke in a calm voice.

The grunt just sat there, scared shitless.

"How come you're only scratched?"

"I just scraped it." Voice quivering, rubbing his thigh. I noticed that his pants were torn, but saw no blood.

"Nobody could catch himself from falling in a damned punji pit."

"He's lying sir. He's had Article Fifteens before, in the states. Always trying to sham."

Captain Ferris glanced from the lieutenant back to the grunt. "You know what malingering is, son?"

Son.

"I didn't do it on purpose."

The captain blew his breath out, shaking his head.

"You want to press charges, lieutenant?"

"Yes, sir."

"All right. Soldier, when you get back from the hospital, you'll go to the mortar platoon. We'll see what happens when the mission's over."

By now the guys on the perimeter were stretching their necks eyeballing. The guy was being accused of malingering, of deliberately scratching himself on a punji stick in order to get out of the boon docks. All punji stick wounds are mandatory dust-offs, regardless of severity. The dinks are said to dip the tips in human excrement, and if the skin is broken you go back to the field hospital. I guess they give you tests and shots.

Phil walked over with the bottle of peroxide still in his hand.

"Other guy's gonna be okay, sir."

"Medevac on the way," said the lieutenant's RTO. Phil nodded and went back to the brother. He and the other medic carried the casualty to the center of the perimeter, laying him before the RTO and me.

Phil told me at lunch that it had entered behind the knee and come out four inches up the thigh, clear of the bone. Had it been two feet longer, it probably would have gone right on into the groin. Punji sticks are razor-sharp bamboo; if you fall, really fall with all your weight, there's no telling what they can do, depending on the angle at which you hit. The brother was conscious and able to talk, but dazed; morphine I guess. It really wasn't that bad, he had hit it on a good angle, but I still don't know why the first platoon hadn't heard him scream. It seems like you'd *have* to scream, though on the other hand punji sticks are so sharp, maybe you don't feel it unless it hits a bone. I don't know.

The other grunt stared at the brother, medics kneeling over him, and screamed at Lieutenant Jackson.

"I didn't do nothin!"

Captain Ferris jerked him by the collar, with everyone watching.

"Shut up, soldier." Actually pulling his ass off the ground, the guy whimpering.

"Sir," still held by the captain, "I been in the field ten months. Why the fuck is he harassin me? Why would I try to fuck myself up?"

Captain Ferris let the collar loose.

"Nobody's court-martialed you yet, soldier. You'll go back and join the 81s. I'll let you know if there's any charges."

The stupid grunt smiled, and that blew it. What's more, he realized he was smiling and immediately straightened his face. Captain Ferris and the lieutenant had both been eyeballing him. They glanced at each other, then back at him.

"It was a booby trap!" shaking his head.

"Shut up." Captain Ferris grit his teeth as he said it and shoved him, sprawling him on his back.

"You're in the goddamned jungle, troop."

The bird's muffling soon became audible, and Lieutenant Jackson popped yellow smoke. The crew chief swung out the penetrator as it hovered.

Dust-off. I guess it had become routine by now. Phil and the other medic lifted the wounded brother into the sling and waved to have him hauled up. The pant-leg was torn off, but the boot and sock still on, sock soaked red with blood as was the wide bandage. The other guy stepped into the sling on his own power, carrying the brother's rifle and pack in addition to his own rifle.

Captain Ferris called in the sit-rep, first reporting the WIA and then the story of the accused malingerer. He referred to both by roster number instead of name.

I doubt if the perimeter could make out the conversation, but they knew what was going on. Especially when the captain had grabbed him, and with the guy's yelling.

Malingering. Nobody liked the bush, but I never saw nor heard of anyone else trying that. He did get justice though, in the fitting way that only the army can give. Instead of charges or a court martial they made him a permanent KP back at base camp. KP, seven days a week, and with gooks. I guess a college bastard would say that there was no proof that he had malingered or that he was denied rights in being made a KP without reference to any crime. Fuck a bunch of college bastards.

Captain Ferris called the first platoon into a huddle before we moved on.

"All right, third platoon just ran into punji sticks, so let's be on guard." He looked at his watch. "Another hour we'll break for chow. We've got an easy route of march, should be in the november lima by three."

I remember that mission as the most pleasant of the entire tour. We never set up any later than three in the afternoon, and wouldn't break camp until eight in the morning. With the dry season and the easy terrain, it was almost fun. The teak woods kept it shady as you walked, and we rarely ran into elephant grass—elephant grass absorbs the heat and is exhausting to push through. In the late afternoon, after setting up, we would sit around, talking and playing cards, some guys smoking and boiling water for hot chocolate—like cowboys on the prairie.

There were only four or five contacts, all of them small, never reaching the gunship phase, let alone air strikes. They seemed routine after Jude.

I never worried about dinks the whole time, the only operation we ever had where I didn't. I can't explain the light-heartedness.

A couple times we would stop at a river and swim for an

hour, one platoon securing while the other two were in. I don't know whether the TOC had deliberately planned our route with such leisure in mind or whether Captain Ferris must said fuck it and took things easy on his own. I like to think he did it on his own. Higher would never deliberately allow time for troops to play around in the bush. On the other hand though, maybe the only thing they really cared about was just keeping us out, *any* place, and making it look on the map as if we were following a mission. Anyway, it's too bad they're all not like that. That was the only one.

That first day we stopped for lunch at a river. I called in the papa lima while Phil mixed my can of beef in spiced sauce with his beans and meatballs. We had heat tabs, and he had stolen a jar of steak sauce and a can of garlic salt from the red legs mess tent. Naturally, he had to pass both bottles around. Even Captain Ferris used it.

"That's some good shit," said Phil.

"Put cheese in it?" asked Captain Ferris.

"No, forgot, God damn it."

"Put a couple cans of cheese in it and you've got some real eatin."

"Better than a mess hall," I said.

"So fuck it," said Phil. "Hardship tour."

We remained there over half an hour after everyone had finished, lying back against the packs, smoking, talking in low tones. With Kell and Lieutenant Chivington we had never spent over twenty minutes for lunch, and always immediately moved out. Phil and I went to the river bank to rinse the canteen cups, then sat together against a big teak wood.

"Wonder what old Fi Bait's doin now," said Phil.

"He's fuckin. Smokin two-dollar cigars."

"Fuckin his balls off. Hey, I wonder if old Shoates goes down today and knocks off a whore."

"The Anachronism? No, he's a fucking Baptist."

"Baptist, shit."

Captain Ferris called me down for consultation, making sure I had the right november lima on my map and showing where the second and third platoons would most likely find anything in their sweeps. There were only two more check points, and the second would be the november lima.

We were set up and lying barefoot in our hootches before three-thirty. Phil and I were again together, Captain Ferris with his RTO. The second and third platoons set up on our flanks. It was more or less one big oblong perimeter. I worked up a delta tango for the 105s and fired it in right on the trail—the november lima was on a slope two hundred meters above a trail. I adjusted it from Sam's and Jacob's machine gun position.

I thought how this would be my first adjustment by sight rather than having to judge by the sound because of the thick canopy. After the smoke round and two HEs I decided to act like a bigshot and let Phil give an adjustment. He gave a left five-zero, drop five-zero and brought it within five meters of the trail. I called in mark target. Phil naturally bragged, and Sam and Jacobs teased me. I never let anyone else play around at FO-ing again.

After the battery had recorded the final adjustment I told the captain, and he sent one squad from the third platoon to set up an ambush on the trail. They took one machine gun and did not set up hootches. If they saw too many dinks for ambush they were to low-crawl back in and I would call in the artillery, though they saw nothing all night. We had no contact for the entire first week, and morale was at a peak.

We found the first dinks sometime during the second week, ninth or tenth day I'd say. Headquarters element itself found them. The point man came running back to the captain and we low-crawled—I'll never forget, *low-crawled* with that damned pack and radio—up to the edge of the hill.

We formed a straight line along the ridge, with the dinks sitting in a ravine directly below us. Sitting ducks. They would have to run uphill, no way to escape. I remember thinking how they had to be crazy or high on dope to stop in a place like that.

There were four, with AK-47s and cloth boony hats. All the weapons and packs were piled up, three feet from the nearest guy. They had a fire going, boiling a small kettle of rice. Sitting in a circle, barefoot, and wearing shorts. One guy had a pistol belt.

Captain Ferris whispered on the radio for the second and third platoons to stop moving and set up perimeters; sit tight, we had dinks and were going to try to take prisoners.

I was right beside the captain, Phil next to me and then Sam and Jacobs with their big sixty.

"We can take them prisoner, Winsted," the captain whispered. Whispered right in my ear and put an arm around my shoulder. "Pass the word, nobody shoots unless you have to."

I jerked back and stared at him. *Prisoners.* I stared at the dinks, snickered at the captain again, and shook my head.

I leaned to Phil like the captain had, only not hugging him. "If they move, *shoot* the fuckers."

Phil nodded without taking his eyes off the dinks and passed it down. Captain Ferris's RTO passed the word to the other half of the line, I don't know what their interpretation was. Prisoners.

We must have lain there two minutes, just watching the dinks. I was almost laughing to myself at the absolute comedy of the situation: there we were, had them right there, and just eyeballing. I also felt a thrill at having given my own order.

I leaned and whispered to the captain. "Can you talk gook, sir?"

I don't know what he had been waiting for. Finally, with my question, he yelled down.

"Chieu hoi, chieu hoi," which is gook for surrender or open arms.

They looked up but didn't have time to respond. I don't know who opened up first; after the first shot everyone was working out except the grenadier, who was at too close range for HE to explode, and I guess he didn't want to waste any cannister rounds. It lasted about a minute. I just used one magazine and stopped. None of them even got near their rifles.

The small black kettle had two holes through it, water and rice streaming out like in the movies. Even Captain

Ferris had fired. Dinks. When it was over he called the other elements and told them we were moving down. He also called the TOC and told them we had made contact.

Captain Ferris was the first down and started searching a body.

"Start the others," looking up at us.

"Christ, those guys are fucked *up,*" said Jacobs.

"Look like little cherubs," I said, "only all fucked up."

Phil and Sam laughed. "Fucking pervert."

"They *do,*" I said, eyeballing Phil.

We had brought the max on them. They really did look like little cherubs, all twisted. Because of the tumbling effect of the M-16 round, whenever a bone is hit it splinters and breaks at an odd angle. Legs and arms limp and twisted. One guy looked like he had three elbows on one arm, another, two knees. One was lying on the rear slope of the ravine, on his side with one arm over his head, just like a little cherub. The other one had taken it in the head, coming out the front, one eyeball dangling, mouth open and the other eyeball staring.

Cherubs. You don't get sick like you're supposed to on the six o'clock news. I guess in the movies the college guy is supposed to be the "sensitive person." Fuck the movies. In the movies I guess I would never have told anyone to shoot. Fucking dinks. Prisoners, shit. I don't know. If you kill one you kill one. They really did look like cherubs. But what are you supposed to do? Tell them to chieu hoi. What about Kell and Mastion. I don't want any hassle. I don't know, sometimes you brood and really do feel like an animal, but what the *fuck?*

We found a map and two documents on one guy, a few hand-written notes on another. I went through one ruck sack and all it had was a white silk shirt and two land crabs. Two land crabs. I jumped back when I found them; Phil and Sam laughed. Dinks are amazing, walking barefoot through the damned jungle with nothing but a rifle and two land crabs.

Everybody took a couple AK rounds for souvenirs. We called for a bird to take the weapons and documents, and the second and third platoons closed. They too went down for AK rounds. We left the bodies in the ravine, formed a perimeter above and smoked and talked while waiting for the bird. Captain Ferris gave the whole company a talk before we moved out.

"Okay men, this is the first dinks we've found, that's a sign we might be gettin near something. It's been a dicked patrol so far, and I've been pretty damned lax. But we're gonna have to be sharp from now on. Watch out especially for snipers."

We didn't hit any snipers. Only four or five brief contacts, more like accidents really. Nothing like a real fire fight, a calculated ambush. The dinks were patrolling the bush just like us, and our paths just happened to cross. Only two American KIAs for the whole mission, and neither one from the first platoon.

After those first four we didn't get any confirmed dink KIAs. We found blood trails each time, but the dinks had dragged the bodies off. It was unlike real dinks to stop in a ravine like those first four had. Must have been high, or maybe even deserters. You never know. I never lost any sleep over it.

I do wonder, though, whether my message to Phil really had been the main thing causing us to shoot or whether someone would have fired anyway. "Chieu hoi." Someone would have shot anyway. Goddamned dinks.

The contacts didn't alter morale either, at least not for the mighty first platoon. I'm sure the second and third were in the dumps when they suffered their KIAs; we were too but not that much.

I would fire in a delta tango every night, and Phil and I kept experimenting with hot sauce and garlic salt menus. In the early evening we would lie barefoot in the hootch and talk about R&R, about girls and the world. How to become a playboy when you go back, a *real* playboy. Then about Fi Bait in Bangkok.

The last day we set up our november lima only a clic from LZ Victory. I let 81s fire the delta tango that night and Fi Bait heard me over the push. He called me after I finished.

I let Phil and Sam both talk to him, and the Anachronism got on with his radio. We talked about two minutes, like television teen-age girls on the telephone. Bubblegum Bob himself called and told us to clear the net.

We walked back into Victory at ten the next morning. Fi Bait was standing there by the wire.

"Hey, motherfucker. How was R&R?"

We shook hands.

"R&R is paradise, motherfucker."

CHAPTER TWELVE

The Anachronism had to be the first person to greet Fi Bait. Uncontrollable grins, back slaps. First question had to be whether or not he'd gotten a blow job, before even saying hello; Fi Bait's only possible reply, "Fucking pervert."

When I asked him that morning at the wire, all he could do was grin and shake his head.

"Wow Henry, I can't describe it. It's just paradise."

Grinning big, "Paradise. You gotta go."

He had had his chauffeur take a polaroid picture of the two of them standing on the hotel balcony. Fi Bait in a blue pin-stripe suit and wide red tie, with his arm around her waist. Naturally, a long dark cigar in his other hand and snickering at the whole goddamned world.

"Jesus Christ," I said.

That's all I could say. She was more beautiful than even the French bitch. Smiling up at Fi Bait with her fingers in his hair. Long legs and a mini-skirt, the straight shimmering black hair to her hips.

"God *damn*, Fi Bait. I can't believe it."

"Don't torture yourself," wrapping it back in plastic as we walked through the perimeter.

"How much was she?"

"Twenty-five bucks a night. But worth it. Make a goddamned good wife. I'm gonna write her a letter. Forget those goddamned college bitches."

"God damn, is she nice," I said.

"If I'd stayed I'd have married her, Henry. That's no lie. I wanted to cry gettin on that plane."

Bangkok. Six nights of heaven. No hassle. That long hair to her hips, the unpretentious smile, lying there with the sheet tucked under her chin when he woke up. Kissing to awaken her; immediately the moaning, and hugging, shifting the firm legs.

"Paradise, Henry, paradise."

The afternoons, lying naked under silk sheets, with the sun glowing through the window; holding her hand and spilling your soul, like in a movie, and you didn't feel stupid or Hollywood doing it.

"Me understand," shifting to her side and touching your face.

"Paradise, Henry, paradise. I've *got* to go back."

"So how's four-deuce?" I asked as we walked.

"Sucks ass, all the way. You should see this sorry lieutenant. You know, technically you're in his charge too."

"I give a shit."

"Bring your shit on over to the FO bunker."

He stopped behind me; I slipped out of the pack and he caught it, putting one arm through and leaning into it as we walked.

"Christ, tomorrow you'll be fire base FO, Henry."

"As if I gave a shit."

The Anachronism lay on top of the bunker, with no shirt on and barefoot, reading the new *Playboy.* Even had sunglasses on.

"Henry boy! Hear you chalked up some more dinks."

"I gotta fill Kell's shoes, keep Kentucky number one."

Fi Bait dropped the pack on the roof and I lay the rifle beside it.

"Gentlemen," I said, "we brought the *max* on these dinks. Fuckers were cookin dinner down in a ravine."

"First platoon didn't take any casualties?" asked Fi Bait.

"No, believe it or not. Two KIAs all together, I didn't know the guys. Hey, you guys got beer and soda?"

Fi Bait ducked into the bunker, they were stacked in an

81 box beside the entrance. The coke foamed and sprayed with the first puncture.

"Wow," said the Anachronism. "She's from mother-fucking Indiana, Fi Bait. How am I supposed to act?"

We looked back, he held up the center-fold, grinning and twitching his eyebrows above the sunglasses.

"Horny," I said.

"Give me Bangkok," said Fi Bait.

"You sorry fucker," said the Anachronism. "I don't know what any bitch could see in you."

"What do you do in four-deuce, Fi Bait?" I asked.

"I don't do a *god*-damned thing, friend."

"And still fuckin complainin," said the Anachronism.

"After Bangkok he's used to the good life. I better shave," I said. "Is First Sergeant Ballard back here?"

"That fucker. He's been made the new base camp first sergeant. Sergeant Skinner is you guys' first sergeant now."

"He's okay," I said.

"Dumb fucker," said the Anachronism.

"Still better'n most lifers."

I finished the coke, removed the helmet liner from my pot and moved out for the water trailer down at the pad. I passed old Sergeant Skinner on my way down.

"Need a shave."

"On my way now, Sarge."

Fi Bait had gone back to the FDC when I returned, I went in the bunker to fix my air mattress and poncho liner. On each side was a row of 81 boxes, shoved together to form a platform off the dirt, almost like a bed. There were even two pegs driven into the center log above, for hanging a rifle. It was cool and quiet. I untied my boots and lay down, hands under the back of my head and mind wandering back to the search and destroy, those four dinks, Fi Bait's girl. I noticed that the Anachronism had put last month's playmate on the ceiling over his air mattress, with engineer's spikes.

I was asleep when he and Fi Bait crawled in, but immediately woke up. Fi Bait slapped my knee and sat next to me; the Anachronism stretched out on his own mattress, and we started talking about Fi Bait's R&R.

"Seven times the first night, Henry. God damn, I never thought I had it in me."

"What, you cherry?" asked the Anachronism.

"I never went all *night* before."

"To hear your 'Lieutenant Fuzz' seven times is substandard."

"That sorry fucker. I can't wait till they bring you in and you have to live with him."

"What?" I said.

"Lieutenant Almond, new four-deuce platoon leader. Talk about a fucking pervert, Henry. Thinks he's hot stuff. Goddamned sex maniac."

"Where's he from?"

"Fucking Pennsylvania. ROTC."

"Fuck me," I said.

ROTCs are invariably the most fucked up officers; the most fucked up individuals in the entire army. College boys, never seen the real army, except for a few weeks at Fort Benning. Most think they're so cool that they should take it upon themselves to bullshit with the troops. They try to talk *at* you like they did their fucking candy-ass college buddies. Then they shine the gold bar when you're not chummy in return. Give me Captain Ferris, anytime.

Fi Bait said he had dropped the entire grand in Bangkok, bought a set of bronzeware for his mother, and a teakwood elephant with ivory tusks for himself. He hadn't done much sight-seeing, but did see the royal palace and golden Buddha—he had to wear a necktie and pull his shoes off to get in some of the temples. He also saw four American movies. He laughed telling about the first night ordering a pizza and eating in bed, going again as soon as it was finished. He didn't get drunk, there was too much living to be done.

You wanted to kick the sandbags as he described sitting by the pool, with a Tom Collins, his girl beside him running her fingers through his hair and a two-dollar cigar in the ash tray.

"Let's go down to the water point after chow," said Fi Bait.

"Might as well," I said. "Hey Anachronism, you knock off any them whores?"

"You gotta be shittin me. I'd like to get one of the coke girls though."

"Coke girls?"

"Yeah. They come from the village every afternoon. You go down and bullshit with them."

"Fifty cents a coke," said Fi Bait, "but what the fuck. It's worth it just to talk and play with the kids."

"Popeye," said the Anachronism.

Guys from Bravo company were headed for the river in groups of two and three before we had even finished eating.

Sam and Jacobs passed. Sam waved and yelled, "Hey, Phi Beta Kappa, come on down. Bring your friends."

"We'll be there."

We took off without checking with anyone. As we walked through the four-deuce area Fi Bait pointed to the FDC bunker.

"My new home, gentlemen."

There was a sign made from the lid of a four-deuce box. "4.2 mortars, High Angle Hell," with a picture of a mortar in one corner, a round coming down on a dink's head on the other side.

There were no whores there this time, just Mama-san and her people, Mama-san sitting in the grass with her legs folded and three baskets before her, smoking, like Mammy Yokum. There were nine or ten kids, counting the three teen-aged coke girls. Four or five guys were in swimming, the others talking with the gooks.

Sam was negotiating with Mama-san for a silver peace-sign necklace, with the .45 still on his hip.

"Fifty cent MPC," he said.

Mama-san laughed and shook her head. Showing the black stub teeth, waving her hands.

"Don't let him cheat you, Mama-san."

"Hey, Phi Beta Kappa. How was Bangkok, sorry fucker?"

"Too good, Sam. Too good."

Mama-san dipped into her basket and leaned forward, nodding at Fi Bait and holding a plastic photo album in her hand.

"No. No need, Mama-san."

She tried me, raising her eyebrows.

"No thanks, Mama-san.",

"Where's Popeye the sailor man?" yelled the Anachronism.

All the kids immediately ran to him, laughing and squealing. The oldest couldn't have been over seven. The Anachronism lay his rifle in the grass and picked up Popeye, picking him up like a father would, throwing him, the kid squealing.

"How you been, Popeye?"

"Bullshit," said the kid, laughing and slapping the Anachronism's nose.

"Hey, hey." The other kids laughed and slapped his legs. "Hey, hey."

Popeye wore a boony cap with a CIB in front, covering his ears and shoved back on his head. The Anachronism pulled it down over his eyes. "No say bullshit, not nice," he told him.

"Bullshit," said the kid, wiggling in the Anachronism's arms and squealing as he pushed the hat back up.

All the kids were barefoot, the boys in shorts and girls in the black silk pajama pants and pastel shirts. White circular oriental straw hats like in the movies. One boy had a blue American Bing Crosby golfer's hat, with the first of the twenty-second crest pinned on the side.

One girl tugged my pant leg, I looked down and she pleaded in the soft voice. "You buy candle?"

Big eyes looking up, and that smile, like Wee Willie Winkie. I knelt and lay my rifle down.

"Candle?" I said.

As soon as I smiled she jerked her head aside, embarrassed I'm sure, twisting side to side. I remember the tingling in my face.

"How much, honey?"

Honey.

"One dollah MPC," pleading again.

"One dollah?"

Nodding, exhaling her breath and turning the head aside again.

I stuck the two candles in my leg pocket. She smiled back as I stood up, then ran to give the dollar to Mama-san.

"Hey Popeye, where's your sister?"

"She bullshit."

"Don't say that," pulling the boony hat.

Another kid pulled my leg and flashed the cigarette sign.

"Me no have."

He kept pulling my pant leg.

"No?" shaking his head.

"Sorry, Pard."

"S'okay, Joe," moving on.

Jacobs sat on the grass bouncing the little boy with the golf hat on his knees. I didn't notice the coke girl approach me; I spun around when she touched my arm.

"You buy coke?"

She was beautiful. Black eyes sparkling and skin soft in the shade of the straw hat. I had never seen a beautiful gook. The whore at the first convoy point had been the best, and she was a whore.

"How much?"

"Fifty cent MPC," she said. Emotionless, removed, marble-eyed, like the kid with my Milky Way at Plei Jan, yet so beautiful, *majestic.*

She opened the can for me as I got the money out.

"Thank you," moving on to Mama-san with the money. Couldn't have been over sixteen or seventeen.

"Sister," said Popeye, pointing at her.

The Anachronism turned and saw her, he too became quiet. She put her basket of cokes down and silently took Popeye from his arms.

"Buy coke?"

He did, as did Fi Bait when she got to him.

"Hey, Fi Bait," said Sam, "I'm gonna take this one home."

He held my candle girl in his arms, bouncing her and she holding the big straw hat with one hand and laughing.

"I know what you mean, Big Sam."

Rather than go swimming we sat on the grass beside Jacobs to watch and talk to the kids. But just as you're feeling good they bring your mind back to the Big V. Second Lieutenant Almond. He came strutting down the trail, strutting, with the gold bar shining on one side of his collar, crossed rifles on the other. He had no head gear, packed a .45; five guys from four-deuce flocked behind him. One was Braxton, a tall brother buck sergeant. Lieutenant Almond had curly blond hair and white teeth. He was probably the handsomest guy I had seen in the Army.

Lieutenant Almond. "Lieutenant Fuzz." ROTC, B.A. in Political Science. Your classic smart-assed college boy. Even from the *East*. When I went into four-deuce, he would come in while I was on radio watch and talk for hours. I had to sit there and listen. He would talk about how many blow jobs he'd had, and of eating them out.

Fi Bait and the Anachronism and I would talk about it only in the abstract, more as a way to pass the time than anything else. How could you talk about *real* girls that way? Brag about how many you had had and how gross you could make them go. He even had pictures, snapshots of them. Naked, and they were beautiful. American college girls.

My God, how I would have loved to shoot Lieutenant Almond, shoot him right between the eyes with an M-16. Tumbling effect. One was a beautiful redhead, standing smiling with her legs spread and holding Lieutenant Almond's penis in one hand. College. His daddy had bought him a Corvette and sent him to Purdue.

"Hey sir, here's your Bravo FO," said Fi Bait.

I didn't move, eyeballing the Hollywood handsome face. Curly blond hair.

"Winsted?"

"Yes, sir."

"Lieutenant Almond. Been fuckin the gooks?"

His father was probably a stock broker, and a junior officer in World War II or something. Playboy. His five four-deuce men hovered behind him on the trail.

My candle girl tugged his pant leg and looked up with the Shirley Temple smile.

"Buy candle?"

"Go way kid, ya bother me," he said laughing.

"W. C. Fields," said Braxton.

"Come back in seven or eight years, kid, I'll let ya use the big dick for a candle."

She stood there still looking up at him.

I was burning, wanting to ram the butt of my sixteen in his teeth.

Four-deuce laughed.

He pushed her back.

"Better luck next time, bitch," said Braxton.

She ran to Mana-san crying. My God. I wanted to hug her. Hands over her face and hidden under the hat as she cried. I wanted to kill him. Not like when you shoot a dink but as an act of will, like a gunfighter. Looking back, that's the only time I ever felt that way. I like to think Fi Bait and the Anachronism had to feel the same way.

"Hey, where's the bastard with the CIB?" yelled the lieutenant.

"There he is, sir," said the brother, pointing.

"Come here, kid."

Popeye approached slowly, and the lieutenant grabbed his boony hat. Popeye kicked at him, but he was barefoot. The lieutenant just laughed at him.

"CIB, I don't have a CIB myself and this little fucker's got one."

"Probably got it from a VC," said Braxton. "Mama's probably a VC whore."

The kid was kicking the lieutenant for all he was worth, screaming, but not crying.

Popeye turned and looked to the Anachronism, but what could *he* do? Second lieutenant. "I don't have a CIB myself." If only someone *would* put him in the jungle, I thought. What I wouldn't give to throw a white phosphorous grenade on him.

He finally threw the boony hat in the river and let Popeye down. Popeye ran down after it crying.

One of the grunts in the water got the hat for Popeye and waded out to give it to him.

"Okay people, listen up," said the lieutenant.

"These gooks aren't supposed to be here." Hands on hips. "You guys keep comin down here every day and playin with 'em and one of these times they're gonna have booby traps waiting. Colonel Fetterman wants all fraternization stopped. A bunch of ARVNs raped some bitch in the village last night and the gooks probably won't appreciate it. So everybody out of the water, start movin back to the wire."

He was trying to sound authoritative, but it didn't come off. With Colonel Fetterman it might have, but even Colonel Fetterman couldn't be animal enough to treat those kids like that.

The swimmers did wade out though, and started dressing. Silence. My face was throbbing, my little girl stood by Mama-san sobbing. Popeye held on to his sister's leg. She stared at the lieutenant with those piercing hollow eyes, like that kid at Plei Jan.

"All right you gooks, di di mau," clapping his hands.

Di di mau is gook for go away, but they just kept staring. He clapped like grandmaw trying to shoo the chickens from under the porch.

"Di di mau, di di mau," waving his arms.

All the Americans stared too.

"Braxton," he finally yelled.

"Yes, sir."

The brother smiled and pulled a CS grenade from his leg pocket. You could tell it was CS by the grey color. The gooks too knew what it was and started gathering their stuff.

"You men hurry up, start movin."

A few gathered their rifles, pots and bandoliers and started walking. The representatives of the mighty first platoon—Sam, Jacobs, Fi Bait, the Anachronism, and me—remained steadfast, sitting in line on the grass.

"You can't CS those people lieutenant," said Fi Bait, in

a straight voice, as he had with Captain Granger at the stand down.

"The *fuck* I can't, troop." Eyeballing Fi Bait. "You guys move out."

We didn't move. Defiance. It felt good.

"Colonel Feterman tell you to CS those people?" asked Big Sam.

"What's your name, troop?"

"Crow."

"Crow *sir.*"

"Crow, *sir,*" said Sam.

ROTC second lieutenant trying to play soldier. Sam just eyeballed him.

The lieutenant stammered. "You guys gonna move out or get CS'd?"

He was going to do it anyway. You were sick to your stomach, but what could you do? We got up together and walked by him in single file, deliberately brushing close and turning our heads to stare at him.

We stopped ten meters up the trail and looked back. The gooks had gathered their things but stood there in a huddle.

"Di di," he said. They kept staring, even the kids.

Braxton walked down to them. The breeze happened to be ideal. He popped the grenade and dropped it five feet in front of them, running back to his lieutenant. With the wind it hit them all; they ran randomly, coughing and screaming, dropping their baskets, little kids crying. I wanted so bad to kill him.

They should have run into the wind, it couldn't get them on the other side of the grenade. But what did a bunch of kids know? The coke girls and Mama-san tried to round them up. The smoke was like the white mist of the Jude monsoon. They were soon out of sight running. But you could still hear the screaming and coughing.

The lieutenant turned to leave the scene, but he stopped seeing the five of us. We stared until he looked away, then walked back to the perimeter.

Lieutenant Almond. I was only in his FDC a month,

thank God. I wanted to kill him so *bad*. "I don't have a CIB myself." College bastards. But what can you do?

The five of us went to the FO bunker and spent the afternoon talking about the Lieutenant Almonds and buck sergeant Braxtons of this world.

"Tell me it ain't a fucked up world," I finally said, to no one in particular.

"I can't tell you," said Sam. "Who was that motherfuckin brother with the lieutenant?"

"Had to be a future lifer," said Jacobs.

"There it is," said Fi Bait. "Sergeant Braxton. Pushin for E-6. He's a squad leader on a gun crew."

We must have talked for two hours, though most of the time we just sat, staring at the dirt floor, enjoying the shared camaraderie.

"Tell Sam how many times you went the first night," said the Anachronism.

"Seven times Big Sam."

"Show 'em the picture," I said.

It really was a great pose, Fi Bait like a big shot in that pin-stripe suit, the cigar, and girl. What a life! But even that couldn't change the mood.

A slick beat in; I picked up the slapping and consciously followed it in. The beats soon became almost indiscernible, shrill humming like a band saw.

I asked Sam if he had felt anything when we killed those dinks on the search and destroy, immediately blushing and cursing myself for having mentioned it.

"Fuck no," his eyes closed. They all had their eyes closed by then, and arms folded.

"Neither did I."

"You can't worry about that shit," said Fi Bait.

"I know."

"God still loves you and has a wonderful plan for your life," said the Anachronism.

"Amen," said Jacobs.

"Mail call!" someone outside yelled.

I got up first, and Fi Bait asked me to get his and the Anachronism's.

SFC Skinner was at the CP passing it out to the squad

leaders. I got my own, since I was *the* Bravo company FO party, lock, stock, and barrel. I didn't even try to hassle looking for Fi Bait's and the Anachronism's; they weren't Bravo company and I knew I couldn't get it. They were pissed off when I returned without it, and both went out.

I was glad to see them go, to be alone with my mail in the cool bunker. I lay back hoping to finish before they returned.

I got a letter from my father, and one from Kell. Fucking Kell. I actually blushed when SFC Skinner handed it to me. I had never thought about him as a friend, as writing a letter. But I was glad to get it, and answered it.

He addressed it "Hey hillbilly."

He was in Japan and would be going back to Kentucky in two months. He said he was getting a discharge, and *glad* of it. That set me back.

"Fuck this army," he said. "what did they ever do for me, except cause harassment and get me fucked up? My mother sent me a paper from home with my picture on the front page telling how I am a fucking hero, Henry. I hope you make it through okay."

I thought back to the eastern Kentuckian in the barracks that first day in base camp—before the lifer image—that flat jutting jaw, and the bulging Adam's apple.

"I can't wait until I can walk again, Henry, because I am going to go back home and work the land with my daddy. I would like some day to leave Harlan County and get me a place of my own in the western part."

That really got me. Kentucky. The western part of the state, where there are no coal mines nor forty-acre dirt farms with mules and fifty-foot burned-out tobacco beds. I thought of our old place on Dry Branch. I hoped that he would make it.

"Henry, I know that not too many guys thought much of me in the platoon but I tried my best. I've been doing much thinking. I am going to send you a care package. Please write."

"P.S. These nurses make a man forget he's in no shape to fuck."

I put it back in the envelope. Saved it.

Fucking Kell. If he hadn't been wounded I'm sure he would have become a lifer, and maybe an alcoholic. We wrote three or four letters to each other; I still have his.

I wonder if he really did leave Harlan County. I hope he did, but the odds are so great against it. Christ, he may even have gone to Detroit or Chicago to work in a factory, like my own daddy.

I never told Fi Bait or the Anachronism that I had heard from Kell. I wanted to keep it personal. That afternoon he became special. Kentucky, *eastern* Kentucky.

I was reading the one from my father and stopped when they returned. Fi Bait got one from the French bitch and translated it aloud. The Anachronism and I naturally stopped him every line with wisecracks.

"I thought you'd jettison her and let me take over after R&R, Fi Bait."

"Shit, she wants *my* dick, Henry. You can have her when I go home, when I won't have no use for her. Hell, I may even give you the picture."

"You think that picture's for real, Fi Bait?" asked the Anachronism. "You think that's really the same bitch that writes the letters?"

"How'd I know?" If I ever get to France I'll let you know."

"Ten to one it ain't her."

"You never know," I said. "The French are notorious for promiscuity and horniness, even the good-lookers."

Fi Bait yawned. "If you're gonna tear down my woman, I guess I'd better go check back with High Angle Hell. Lieutenant Fuzz is probably lonesome for my company."

"See you at chow, Fi Bait," said the Anachronism.

I lay back down, thinking of Kell and eastern Kentucky—the freight rolling over the trestle at Hayes Crossing on its way to Ashland, thirty-seven coal gondolas, crossing the bridge at Maysville in the old Packard when we would go back down to visit on Memorial Day, the river muddy brown and a red barge train with little white boat churning behind, pushing on up to Portsmouth.

Poor Kell. At least his mind was unfucked about the

army. I couldn't go back to Kentucky, not by myself. What could I do down there?

After supper the Bravo company brothers formed their singing group, joined by a few brothers from Alpha company. I requested "Hey Jude" but it wasn't like before. Not like Jude, with our table, and Cambodia in the background.

Sam and Jacobs stood with them, in the outer ring, but neither joined in singing. I thought back to the stand down with Sam singing "Lonesome Valley" like Leadbelly.

We lay on top of the bunker on into the sunset, the swelling orange ball, no clouds.

"Sixty days' hump tomorrow, what a fucking bummer," said the Anachronism.

"Least you won't have your red leg FO to hassle you," said Fi Bait.

"Got a gung ho CO though."

"It's a hardship tour."

It was dark wtihin an hour, the stars actually sparkling and just enough moon to silhouette the wood line.

"Fuck," said the Anachronism, "I'm gonna toke up." He lay in the middle; Fi Bait and I immediately looked at him.

"Christ, you carry it around in your pockets?" asked Fi Bait.

"Why the fuck not?"

The joint was already rolled, and he offered me one.

"Can't be usin it," I said.

"Fuck it, Henry. Can't knock it if you ain't tried it."

"Get busted."

"Shit," said the Anachronism. "What are they gonna do, send me to Vietnam? Put me in the infantry?"

I was thinking about what would happen if a lifer came around. We were all quiet as he smoked.

I jumped when the star cluster went, low-crawled back against the sandbags, heart throbbing. When a star cluster goes there is a whoosh like a pinwheel on the Fourth of July, then five seconds before it pops in the sky. Those five seconds, staring into the sky, not knowing, waiting for the color, waiting for a mortar round to fall on your head. I held my hands in the position for doing pushups.

It popped green, streamers fanning, everyone yelling and running to fighting positions. Green star cluster, one-hundred-percent alert.

Fi Bait took off for the FDC, the Anachronism went in and threw out our rifles, handing out his radio. The 81s popped perimeter illumination as the two of us ran to the TOC. Rounds bursting high on each side of the perimeter, soft candle glow and the plastic sandbags glistening as if wet. I felt like John Wayne, running with the rifle, people scrambling around me, mortar tubes popping.

There were two guards at the CP's concertina and they gave us the password and waited for the counter-sign, flak jackets on and rifles at port arms.

"You gotta be shittin me," sid the Anachronism. We shoved between them, trotting to the bunker.

Inside Captain Ferris and Colonel Fetterman stood by an easel map, both smoking cigars; calm and talking behind the grinding generators. We went to the artillery liaison table.

"What the fuck is it?" asked the Anachronism. "You want some rounds brought in?"

"No, there's an ARVN company in contact."

It was Bubblegum Bob himself. I would have recognized the voice anywhere. I had pictured him as skinny, but he must have weighed two-fifty, with crew cut and eyeglasses, a white undershirt, and the sweating belly rippling.

"So they just got us on alert because of that?"

"Roger, no big gig. They're about a click out."

Roger.

I saw SFC Skinner walk in, must have just finished checking the bunker line. Flak jacket and CAR-15.

"Sarge," I said.

He came to us and touched my arm.

"Oh, Winsted. You two FOs, go to the fightin trench along the river side. Keep your radio turned on. It's just an alert, but maybe we'll need you. Okay?"

"Right, Sarge," said the Anachronism. "How long you think it'll last?"

"Who can say?"

Outside the 81s were popping continuous illumination, two new rounds up before the other two had burned out and the entire perimeter glowing. Four-deuce and the 105s were firing missions, blocking fire for the ARVNs. We walked calmly across the perimeter. If you looked directly at an illumination round you could see the little parachute floating down as it started to burn out. I watched one, even though I knew the glare would ruin my night vision.

The trench was armpit deep, two feet wide. We jumped in ten feet from the nearest guys on either side of us.

"Fuck, I bet they keep us up all night," said the Anachronism. He set the radio on the dirt ledge before the sandbags, turned it off "squelch" so we could hear all the traffic.

You could hear Fi Bait taking adjustments from Bubblegum Bob on the radio. Bob apparently had another radio on the gook's push and had someone translating.

"Fucking CO'll probably get us up at five-thirty in the morning before we move out."

"It don't mean nothin," I said.

Pretty soon Bubblegum Bob gave four-deuce and 105s a check fire; gunships and Snoopy on their way.

"All *right,*" said the Anachronism. "You're gonna see a show. Fuckin Snoopy brings the max."

Snoopy is an airplane—a C-something—with four sets of mini-guns.

It carries enough ammunition to give continuous fire for an hour or so, 6,000 rounds per minute from each gun. While we waited for the show the 81s cut the perimeter illumination to just one round every two minutes. The Anachronism pulled another joint from his pocket.

"Wanna toke up, Henry?"

"No," looking at the river.

"What's the matter, you still a fucking Baptist?"

"I don't need the shit."

"Fuck," he said.

The Cobras arrived first, Bubblegum Bob gave the 81s a check fire on the illumination and we heard them beat in, turned our heads as they lanced over the perimeter. There was a red light on the bottom of each but with your night vision impaired from the illumination nothing else visible.

We followed the lights across the river. I don't know how they determined exactly where the ARVNs were; the gooks probably had flashlights pointed straight up or something. We saw the two red dots split and circle, then the rocket pods bursting pink and the chilling shrieks—thoong, thoong—as the rockets slammed in, red streamers behind their paths, explosions flat in the distance. The yellow flash of the mini-gun followed, red tracers and that electric rip like a bum microphone. There are five ball rounds between each tracer but you could see nothing but a solid thin streak of red, steady rip. Then quiet, the rotors slapping muffled as they circled for the next pass.

We watched in silence, the Anachronism blowing the joint. They stopped after three passes and left, streaking over us again.

Snoopy started before the Cobras were out of ear-shot, spitting four red ribbons as he circled their perimeter, one round hitting every twelve inches along each gun's line of fire. He worked out for half an hour. He would stop occasionally, give short bursts a few times, almost like a rifle. After he left, all was quiet, even our perimeter illumination stopped. The Anachronism was on his third or fourth joint by then.

"Some alert," I said.

"Fucking joke. If the dinks hit, you'll hear popcorn before any fucking star cluster."

They kept us on alert until one in the morning. Every thirty minutes the 81s would pop one illumination round on general principle, probably just to keep us awake. After Snoopy, the medevacs came in for the ARVNs. Four of them, each with the strobe light beaming straight down into the bush, a thick, white beam reminding you of an automobile show room. All you could see were the beams, but you knew they were medevacs. Hovering in line, one turning off the light and moving out as the next moved up.

As the Anachronism got higher he started his old rap, the Baptists and what a fucked up world it was. I didn't want to hear it, was annoyed, and disgusted with the acrid smell. But I would grunt and make conversation when he demanded. I didn't want the hassle of him making a scene.

"What's it mean, Henry?"

"Nothin, John." looking at the river.

"What are we gonna do when we get back? Fuckin hippies, fuckin protestors. Fucking VFW. Who's gonna understand? Who's gonna give a fuck?"

"You gonna smoke goddamned marijuana when you get back."

"Wow. Henry," shaking his head, "What do you wanna come down hard on me for? You and fucking Fi Bait. God *damn* it."

"You'd better keep it down."

"*Fuck* it. What am I gonna do, Henry? I don't wanna smoke fucking marijuana. I ain't no goddamned hippy. I'm a fucking *Baptist.*"

He kept on, about how he could never fit in society, how his mind and values had been destroyed.

I wished Fi Bait were there. I was pissed off. I understood how he felt, *I* felt that way, but to see someone pitying himself and whimpering like a goddamned kid. I don't know. Marijuana. Self-pity. Fucked up world. Fortunately he went right to sleep when we got back to the bunker. I signed off the radio for both of us.

CHAPTER THIRTEEN

I guess that night was the prelude—indeed, the omen. Hollywood could say that everything had been progressively building. Whores, four dinks, CS. Anachronism. But fuck Hollywood.

That very next morning, everything, *everything* collapsing and hitting my brain at once, before I could comprehend anything.

"I ain't kiddin, God damn it! You guys are both goin out, right away."

The guy was squatting at the entrance, yelling. I lay on my stomach and played possum, snuggled in the poncho liner with the sun glowing through the 81 box windows.

"You guys hear me? You awake?"

"Who the fuck are you, Pal?" muttered the Anachronism. Muttering as a drunk awakened with a hangover.

"TOC RTO. A loach spotted some dinks in the open, you guys are CAin right now."

"Right now, my ass," said the Anachronism.

I snuggled in the warm poncho liner.

"I'll just have to tell the Colonel."

The Anachronism sat up, rubbed his eyes, "Who the *fuck* do you think you are?" and threw a boot at him.

"Hit the goddamned road," I yelled.

"Hit the road!" yelled the Anachronism.

He had polished boots, but the sun was behind him as you looked up and I couldn't make out his features.

"I'm a Spec-Five."

I threw a boot, hitting his arm.

The guy left holding both arms in front of his head for protection. We looked at each other and laughed, then lay back down.

I chuckled looking at the playmate spiked to the ceiling, but at the same time unavoidably thinking of what he had said, of CAing that morning.

"Goddamned commandoes," mumbled the Anachronism. He had rolled back onto his stomach and pulled the poncho liner over his head. I looked at my watch; it was seven-thirty, and we should have been up and shaved by now. I was pulling my boots on when Captain Ferris came.

"All right, God damn it."

He spoke with *authority.* The Anachronism threw back his poncho liner.

"You guys get your goddamned asses out to that pad."

"Just dressing now, sir," I said.

"Dressin shit. You both be down at that pad with radios and fighting gear in five minutes for a briefing. Understand?"

"Yes, sir," said the Anachronism.

"Yes sir, shit," said the Anachronism after the Captain left. "Goddamned army. Let me see that fucking RTO, see if I don't shove a goddamned M-16 down his throat."

"Ram it up his goddamned ass," I said. "CA." Tightening the boot laces.

"Somebody probably saw a water buffalo or somethin, Henry."

We strapped our radios in the packs and set them against the wall outside. We tossed out the pistol belts and pots, carried the rifles, pistol belt heavy with grenades and magazines, always clinging low at the hips. The pack was unbelievably light with nothing but the radio—a PRC 25 only weighs twenty-five pounds.

I walked five feet behind him, I remember him swaying, stooped over, his rifle dangling by the suitcase handle. He had two bandoliers, criss-cross on his chest and tied in back. I had only taken one, and it had only four magazines. It was tied around my waist above the pistol belt, like a carpenter's nail apron.

"Hurry up, you guys," yelled the lieutenant. I guess he

had seen our antennas flapping as we approached and knew we were his boys. When he yelled the grunts all turned and watched us.

"Hurry up, shit," muttered the Anachronism.

There were only ten guys, plus the lieutenant. Sam and Jacobs were the only ones I knew besides the Anachronism. Only the RTO had a pack; the others just had pistol belts with dangling grenades, and bandoliers. The riflemen and machine gun teams had criss-crossed machine gun belts on their chests. Sam's big sixty was set up on the ground with the bipod, black barrel gleaming in the sun.

"You guys think this is a goddamned joy ride?" asked the lieutenant. He was short, almost as short as Kell, but stocky, with thick neck and no brogue. We passed him without answering. I deliberately looked away from him, and joined Sam at the rear of the huddle.

"All right, men." He was a second lieutenant. Alpha company I guess, carried a CAR-15.

"Red leg aerial observer says he spotted some dinks an hour ago, south of that ARVN company that got hit last night. They want it checked out, and we're in. Gonna be two birds, I want one FO and one sixty and one seventy-nine on each. It might be a hot LZ. FOs, come here with your maps."

I pulled my map out of the leg pocket as we walked up to him.

"Where's your map?" he asked the Anachronism.

"I didn't bring it."

"You didn't bring it?"

"They just said fighting gear and body."

"What good is an FO without a map?"

"No fucking good at all."

The lieutenant eyeballed him.

"No good at all *sir.*"

"No good at all *sir.*"

Slicks were beating in before the lieutenant could harass him any more or make him go back and get a map—even before he could show *me* where we were going on the map.

"All right," looking at his watch, "this is it. Expect the

worst. Expect a hot LZ. I'm on the first bird; if it's cold, we'll regroup and then recon in two separate teams."

They always told you to expect a hot LZ. It didn't upset you after a time; only the real thing could. I hunched my shoulders to throw the pack higher on my back. The lieutenant divided us, touching a shoulder and nodding which group to join.

The Anachronism went with him, on the first bird. I was with Sam and Jacobs on the second. The Poncho Villa machine gun belts gleamed just like the six o'clock news back in the world.

"Great way to start the morning, ain't it?" asked Sam. He heaved the big sixty, a folded towel on his shoulder for a cushion, balancing the barrel with two fingers.

"Great," I said. "I thought I was gonna sham for thirty days."

"You know better than that," said Jacobs.

We turned our backs against the back wash, holding the pots to our heads, shirt tails flapping below the pistol belts. I ended up on the side, right in front of the door gunner and with my legs dangling.

The door gunner leaned over and yelled in my ear, "How many days?"

"Seventeen lifetimes," I screamed into his face.

"Try three-five and a wake up."

Flying over the village you could see the yellow flag on one of the roofs, like Plei Jan, and a fighting trench before the rice fields. The Anachronism was directly opposite me, legs dangling and kicking like a kid on a swing. He flashed the peace sign; I smiled and held my rifle like Geronimo.

It couldn't have been over a two-minute ride. I was still watching the terrain when the Anachronism's bird floated ahead and dropped. I chambered a round and shrugged my shoulders under the pack, preparing, scooting forward and touching the skid. Our bird hovered behind the other, our pilot watching the lead bird's insertion. Then we dove in like a Cobra, tree-top level, the nose jerking back up as it hovered over the LZ.

Sam and I jumped together, almost choreographed, both hitting on our feet and running for the wood line. The explosion must have gone the instant we jumped. I heard nothing because of the shrill vibrating and grinding of turbine and rotors.

I remember smiling at first, feeling proud of my jump, hitting and immediately running with rifle at high port, like you're supposed to. I saw the Anachronism right off but didn't know it was him. He jerked his head and arms in spasm, three times. As I ran I didn't realize it was him, couldn't imagine it.

But I did know something had happened. Gulping and squeezing the rifle's hand guards, handset flapping against the strap of my ruck.

The lieutenant was spread on his back—chest and face solid red, *solid*, the bandoliers blown apart. His arms and legs were stretched at symmetrical angles. The Anachronism too was dead by the time Sam and I got there. He was in a stranger's arms, one ear gone and the mouth bleeding and gaping, like in a goddamned movie, blood thick in his hair and head limp, right cheek against the shoulder. The throat was orange. The guy rose to his knees, shifted the body, and lay it down. He wiped his bloody hands on his pants. His cross-slung machine gun rounds were stained with blood.

I stood there, crying, seeing him twitch and flail, trembling as I gazed, too numbed to think or even want to curse.

It had been a 105 booby trap, the round wired to a tree and a trip cord at the wood line. The lieutenant's RTO was also dead and the other three on that bird all wounded. It's funny though, none of us even thought about dinks still being around.

I trembled. His throat was *orange*. Nausea spreading, full reality creeping in. The *Anachronism* was *dead*. I knew I was going to puke, but Sam put his hand on my shoulder and told me to call for help. If he hadn't done that, I would have probably ended up bawling like a kid. *Orange*. His eyes were even open.

With Sam's words I forced myself to function, to call for dust-offs. I handed Sam my rifle and pulled out the map as I unhooked the handset. I didn't know where the fuck we were. I took out the compass for a resection. I was feeble, stomach quivering.

"Mauler four-seven, this is eight-four-niner, over."

"Roger, eight-four-niner, send traffic."

It was Bubblegum Bob.

The second slick must have seen the explosion and himself called for dust-offs. He circled as I talked and finally came back in, setting down, and one door gunner charging out with his .45 drawn and his green plastic helmet and visor shining. He saw the bodies, saw the others tending the three wounded, me on the radio, and ran back without speaking. The slick lifted off and circled until medevacs came, then tooks its original passengers back to Victory.

"God, get us some help, just get us some help."

The pulse in my cheeks again, shivers as I talked. "Four-two-eight is a kilo-india-alpha."

"Say again eight-four-niner."

"Say again, four-two-eight, kilo-india-alpha." Choking and stammering.

Fi Bait heard and got on the push.

"Henry." He used Henry, right over the air. "Are you all right?"

"Roger."

Flitting the eyelashes. Like in a fucking movie.

The first dust-offs medics ran out with canvas medical bags and treated the three surviving wounded. All three had somehow missed getting it in the face or chest. The others from our bird had applied standard field dressings while I stood there. One of the three wounded was the guy who had held the Anachronism. He had shrapnel in his left arm.

The Anachronism was the first one they carried away on the KIA bird. One ear gone. They searched the pockets before taking him, Jacobs knelt by one of the medics and got something from him. Head tilted to the side as he was carried off, one guy on the feet, one at the armpits. They brushed past me.

Fucking Anachronism. Jacobs put the lighter in my hand without speaking and went back for the rifle and radio.

WHEN I DIE BURY ME FACE DOWN, SO THE WHOLE WORLD CAN KISS MY ASS.

I didn't even notice the lieutenant when they took him, even though he was the goriest, no face or chest at all, just Hollywood blood; he must have been first into the wood line.

I was still in a daze as we ran to the slick, but now trying to snap myself out. You're in the Big V. It don't mean nothin. You've seen one you've seen 'em all; it's a fucked up world.

I sat with my legs dangling, staring down at the terrain, the trees like dyed cotton balls. I stared marble, hollow-eyed, like the kid at Plei Jan with my milky way. Tears dried on my cheeks, throat tight and swollen.

Fi Bait was waiting at the pad for us. He didn't look at me, squinted into the backwash and slipped the radio off my back. The bird took off and left that frail vacuumed silence.

"My God, Henry," the voice hoarse.

I didn't reply. I knew I would cry.

"Lieutenant Almond wants you to report to him, Henry."

I stopped.

"What can I say, Henry?" He looked away to the bleached dirt. His eyes were red and his face drawn.

Lieutenant Almond sat alone in the FDC, panelled walls with four-deuce lids, playmates of the months tacked all over and two of the lieutenant's own color snapshots above the plotting board.

He rose as we entered. Smoking a cigarette, curly blond hair.

"Winsted. Sit down," extending his arm.

I sat in the RTO chair, holding the steel pot in my lap and rifle between my legs. Pistol belt still on, grenades clanking on the metal folding chair.

"What the fuck happened out there?"

"I don't know."

None of us spoke for a long time. There was a Fifth Dimension song on the radio, a few red leg transmissions on the PRC 25 interrupting.

"Fuck me," the lieutenant said.

I looked up. Cigarette in his mouth and hands on hips.

"Fi Bait, how many other fuckin FOs have we lost as KIAs?"

"Sir, his body's entitled to an escort back to the world," said Fi Bait.

"Escort?"

"Yes, sir."

Captain Granger entered, stooping as he came down the dirt steps. All three of us turned and eyeballed.

"Leave us alone for a while, lieutenant."

"Yes, sir."

Captain Granger reached to the ammo box shelf above me and turned off the transistor radio. Then adjusted his wire-framed glasses, eyeballing me—I could feel it—and sat on the edge of the lieutenant's cot. Fi Bait sat beside him.

"How did he get it, Winsted?"

He was the Cold Warrior New Frontiersman again, like back at the Old Regulars' Inn, with the damned self-confidence, and sympathy.

"I don't know, sir. Booby trap. He was a mess."

He nodded, cleared his throat, and dropped his head, silently tapping the fingers together between his legs. Then standing and pacing. He leaned over the plotting board and looked at the lieutenant's snapshots. Two naked smiling co-eds.

"Jesus Christ, whose the fuck are those?"

"Just two of your amorous platoon leader's conquests," said Fi Bait.

"Fucking Lieutenant Fuzz."

Pacing again, hands on his hips, shined boots.

"It's always bad when you're close to a guy, Winsted. I know, you try but you can't avoid getting your mind messed up."

Fucking Hollywood paternalism. I wanted to turn the radio back on.

"Sir, I've got a letter," said Fi Bait.

"Letter?"

Fi Bait pulled the wallet from his breast pocket and unfolded the plastic bag, pulling the letter from one of the plastic picture holders and carefully unfolding the pale blue USO stationary. Throat swollen almost as tight as Kell's Kentucky Adam's apple as he handed it to the captain.

The captain read it, looked at Fi Bait, sat back down on the cot and read it again.

"What can I say Fi Bait?" Refolding it, looking down. "I'll see the colonel."

"See the colonel, shit. I've got a right, sir."

Actually calling him sir.

"I know, but the thing could have been more appropriately worded."

"Worded, shit."

"Let me talk to him. Did you give one to Shoates?"

"Yes, sir. We did them when we first got to Jude."

"Well. Should be in his personal effects at Clarissa."

I had been watching them, the letter, but I wasn't curious. Totally removed, that sublime relief of total exhaustion as when I let myself collapse in the mud at the end of the first day in the jungle. It had all happened so fast, like in a movie. Anachronism, *dead*. Only last night at my side and talking about the Baptists. Only last night, the first time I had seen him since stand down.

"Well. Might as well see the colonel now. You come too, Winsted."

Lieutenant Almond had been leaning over the blast wall, had probably heard every word. No one spoke. He went back into his FDC, and I heard the transistor radio go on.

I felt odd having the fighting gear still on as we walked to the TOC. We passed two guys burning a barrel of shit, stirring it with an engineer stake. Phil stood with them, probably checking to see that it was all burned through—that's one of the fire base medic's responsibilities. Phil looked at us; I only saw him sidelong and didn't turn.

Captain Granger closed the gate behind and said to wait outside the bunker until he called. I unbuckled the pistol belt; Fi Bait untied the bandolier for me. We both propped our knees up and looked down at the bright yellow dirt as we sat.

"What was the letter, Fi Bait?"

He took the wallet out and carefully removed the letter without speaking.

It was on USO stationery, printed in black ink and folded in quarters, a small hole worn into the center.

"If you have discovered my body, fuck you."

That was the opening.

> I, John Chalmers Shoates, do decree on this third day of March, 1968, that Steven B. Pierce shall escort my dead body back to Indiana if I am killed in action in Vietnam.
>
> I further declare that I am a disillusioned cynic and authorize said Steven Pierce to request that no military religious service be performed over my body by any chaplain. If I am killed in Vietnam, *fuck*you. I don't want any funeral in Indiana either, but my Baptist mother would shit, so no hassle, I still respect her. I also wish to be buried face down, but am sure I won't be. The whole world can still kiss my ass though.

It was signed and witnessed by Sam, like a legal document. I read it twice.

"Holy shit," I said as I refolded it. "Was he stoned when he wrote that?"

Fi Bait grabbed the letter from me.

"No." Slipping it into his pocket.

"I'm sorry," I said. Blinking my eyes and looking at him.

He smiled. "We were half-joking when we did it—you can tell—but he meant it, every word."

It suddenly hit me that the letter meant that Fi Bait would be leaving, probably gone a month. I didn't *want* him to leave, felt the tears forming again. Everything happening, I don't know.

"Do they really have to let you go back, Fi Bait?" Controlling the emotion, watching my hand rub in the yellow dirt.

"We'll soon find out, I guess."

"Fucked up world."

"Jacobs gave me his lighter, Fi Bait. Got it from the dust-off. You want it?"

"No. You keep it. I'm gonna keep the letter."

"Thanks." Wanting to cry again. I made figure eights in the dust I had loosened by rubbing the ground.

"Okay, Winsted, Pierce."

Captain Granger extended his hand as we rose.

"Give me the letter, Pierce."

We both brushed the seats of our pants. I took the rifle and pot but left the rest lying in the dirt.

Colonel Fetterman sat in a folding chair by the easel map. John Wayne.

But this time wasn't like the briefing after Lieutenant Chivington and Fleming's funeral. He was relaxed, actually reminded me of a college professor sitting there with his legs crossed. Without the steel pot he was nearly bald, deep wrinkles at the sides of his eyes.

"Which one of you is Pierce?"

"I am, sir."

The colonel eyeballed Fi Bait and extended his hand for Captain Granger to give him the letter.

He read it slowly, grunted when he finished, shifted in the chair, and looked back up at us. Generators were grinding in the background.

"Was this letter written as some kind of joke, Pierce?"

"No, sir," Fi Bait stammered, hands behind his back at formal parade rest, just like at Fort Polk. Meek. Soldier. "The main thoughts were real."

"Real, eh?"

He spoke softly, but with looming authority.

"Thoughtful of him," smiling and eyeballing Fi Bait. "Did you make one for him, too?"

"Yes, sir."

"Of course you did," nodding. Still holding the letter, and the smile.

"He may have been sarcastic, sir, but he had a right . . ."

"Right, shit," interrupting without raising his voice and

still smiling, staring right at him. "Captain Granger, can you vouch that this letter is authentic?"

"Yes, sir."

The colonel didn't take his eyes off Fi Bait. Small blue eyes.

"So you get a vacation, Pierce. Well done, troop."

He glanced at the letter, extended it for the captain to take.

"I'm sure your buddy will rest easy."

You might have expected Fi Bait to get defiant, but this was the *colonel*. John Wayne. The Anachronism was dead anyway, and it would have only intensified the obscenity to press a scene over it. I don't criticize Fi Bait. On the other hand I guess Colonel Fetterman himself could have gone all the way. He could have told us outright what he thought of anyone who would write such a perverted letter, or of anyone who would try to capitalize on it.

"What about the funeral, sir?" Fi Bait asked.

"Oh, I guess he was serious about the funeral, too?"

"You're college, aren't you?"

"Yes, sir."

"I knew it," nodding and smiling. "had to be. Bet your friend was too."

"Yes, sir."

Colonel Fetterman looked away for the first time, to the map.

"In my day a guy took pride in his education and values. I'm college, Pierce. Believe it or not. OCS in the Korean War. You apply for a commission?"

"No, sir."

"Of course not. Too goddamned spoiled and self-pitying. Love generation." Clearing his throat and pointing at Fi Bait. "There *will* be a funeral, Pierce. His dogtags say he was a Baptist. It's only fitting and proper, for morale."

"But he didn't want one, sir."

"But he's dead. Huh, you're college; you read his fuckin letter. You know a funeral's only a joke anyway." Pause. "Don't you?"

"It was his wish, sir."

"Oh, his wish. You a young man of principle? Did you

know your buddy had his pockets full of marijuana when he died?"

Fi Bait replied immediately, "I had a drill sergeant at Fort Polk who lived off Jim Beam."

Captain Granger brought himself to speak, clearing his throat first.

"Shoates was a fine FO, sir."

The colonel kept staring at Fi Bait; those wrinkles at the eyes narrowed. He uncrossed his legs. Spit-shined jungle boots.

"There will be a funeral, Pierce, and if you weren't leaving with the cadaver you *would* attend. Your other buddy there will represent you." He spoke softly, smoothly.

"Get out of here. All three of you."

Captain Granger led the way.

Just like that.

The captain turned to Fi Bait.

"Pierce, I . . ."

Before that day I had never heard him call Fi Bait by his last name.

"May I have the letter, sir?" holding his hand out.

The captain gave it to him, reflection flashing on the glasses as he turned his head and left. Captain Granger, ex-Green Beret, shut down on his New Frontier premises. But what *could* he do? He was in the army, he had to cover his own ass. You knew he felt low, cowering away from us. Looking back, I like to think that he ultimately resigned his commission.

Fi Bait picked up my pistol belt and bandolier and we went to the FO bunker. I remember looking down at the yellow ground as we walked. Numbed, wanting to shake my head and scream, or something. At the same time trying to think of something to say, feeling so self-conscious. The silence and the flashing images were still tingling my face. The silence and self-consciousness maddening, the images whirling. Only yesterday . . .

"Was the Anachronism a virgin?" I asked.

I don't know why the fuck I said that.

"No, told me he had a girl from his junior year up until he graduated. Said she gave him blow jobs."

I pictured the Anachronism doing it with a blonde, or the lieutenant's smiling redhead. So there are no real Baptists after all, I thought, picturing myself as the only innocent in all RVN, and not wanting to *die* that way,

That afternoon Alpha company left on their search and destroy. Without an FO party. I watched them file by, stooped forward under the packs.

Fi Bait left for base camp to pick up orders and meet the body that afternoon. I escorted him to the pad.

"Maintain your cool, FO," shaking my hand, raising the rifle like Geronimo as the slick lifted off, no passengers but him.

Lieutenant Almond had Sergeant Braxton come to the FO bunker to take away the Anachronism's poncho and air mattress.

I lay in the bunker all that afternoon. Didn't even eat. The Anachronism *dead* and Fi Bait gone back to the world with his body. Wanting to cry, *wanting* to, but unable. Killing, dying, fucking. Anachronism. Colonel Fetterman. Captain Granger. Dinks, college, Kell, Mastion. College girls, Baptists, Kentucky. What the *fuck?*

I tried to mourn for the Anachronism and yet realized for the first time that I didn't know what mourning was, unless it was only the purely biological reflex immediately after something happened. That wasn't enough; I wanted to feel something, some gush of emotion, the same frustration as after killing the first dink, trying to figure it out. I couldn't, I just couldn't. I lay there, all the images, everything at once, numbed.

At the same time pissed off at myself for feeling any emotion at all. All of it, everything I had seen, felt, done; it meant nothing. I had learned that, so why hassle my brain? Yet I knew even then that I would be hassled the rest of my life, like a goddamned movie character. Face down, motherfucker.

Now that it's over I can look back and just shake my head at everything. Vietnam. One of Our Boys. Something to tell the grandchildren—I guess I'm actually a living instrument of death, or something. I still sulk, but have resigned to being that way for good. Fucked up world. Kell. Anachronism. Self-pity.

The chaplain performed his funeral service with all of Echo company in attendance. Echo company, ninety-nine percent of Echo company didn't know who the Anachronism was. "Taps," on the plastic tape recorder. I sat alone on the yellow dirt, in back of four-deuece, thinking of the Anachronism's Uncle Malcolm, the Alamo Scout and Baptist preacher.

Graves registration at Pleiku, plastic body bag with a zipper. Fi Bait on the plane home with the remains. Staring hollow-eyed at the chaplain. CMH, coffin with metal handles.

After the chaplain left, a slick brought out three new cruits. I noticed the brand new jungle boots as they approached from the wire. They walked smartly, straight-backed under the new nylon ruck sacks. One carried a grenade launcher, the others sixteens. No sunburn. I rubbed my hands across the yellow dirt and watched as they were briefed by SFC Skinner, outside the CP's concertina.